Forest for the Trees & Other Stories

Mathieu Cailler

Published by Hidden Peak Press

December 10, 2023

Parker, Colorado

HiddenPeakPress.com | @HiddenPeakPress

Manufactured in the United States of America

Cover Photograph: Jakob Wencek

Author Photograph: Christine Donlon

To Christine, Patrizia, and Alain,
my forever light

CONTENTS

FOREST FOR THE TREES
& OTHER STORIES

Mathieu Cailler

"The heart of another is a dark forest, always, no matter how close it has been to one's own."

—Willa Cather, from *My Ántonia*

THE FATHER

Father Dyer stood at the lectern, then paced in front of the crucifix, the hot lights burning through his thick alb. He stared at the sea of faces that begged him for guidance, examined the desperation in their expressions, and knew that they needed his one-hour Mass to make sense of the six days prior.

"Good morning." His deep voice bellowed through the pews. "I would like to invite all here to take a moment trusting in the Lord to ask for forgiveness of our sins."

Many priests bowed their heads but only counted to five or ten. That was what Father Dyer had been told in seminary—repent on your own time, in Mass, just *one* one-thousand, *two* one-thousand. But today, on a sunny Easter Sunday, Father Dyer folded his hands and closed his eyes. "I have sinned," he said under his breath. "It was a long time ago, but I have sinned. Please guide me."

When Father Dyer brought his head up, many parishioners were already looking quizzically at him, even turning their heads from side to side, tacitly confirming with one another that this portion had gone on for longer than the so-called moment.

He cleared his throat and led the Confiteor: "I confess to almighty God, and to you, my brothers and sisters, that I have sinned . . ."

***

Two days prior, on Good Friday, Father Dyer had sat in his office revising his sermon. He was to head the ten a.m. Easter Mass, only the eighth time he'd lead

15

the congregation in his year and a half at St. John the Baptist Parish.

It wasn't customary for parochial vicars to lead Easter Mass, but Monsignor Broussard was eager to see what the young priest could do. According to Monsignor, Father Dyer "had a way about him, a wonderful blend of wisdom and compassion."

Father Dyer rested in his office chair and listened to a gust of wind push a tree branch against his office window. The branch reminded him of a Bible verse: "All the tithe of the land, whether of the seed of the land or of the fruit of the tree, is the Lord's: it is holy unto the Lord." Sunshine then streamed through the window and exaggerated the amber hues of his desk and wooden floors.

Footsteps neared, stopping outside his office. Father Dyer stared at the thin strip of light between the floor and the door. "Come in," he said. No movement. "Please come in," he said again. He watched the brass knob turn, the polished metal glinting in the soft sunlight.

Before Father Dyer had a chance to identify the person, she said, "Patrick . . . Oh, my God! Oh, sorry, can you say 'God' in a place like this?"

"Beth!" he said, pushing out his office chair. He laughed. "Yes, yes, of course. He understands."

Beth wore a fashionable navy skirt with a white blouse that was unbuttoned enough to see her prominent collarbones. Her blue eyes, as always, were surrounded by a heavy coat of eyeliner, and clusters of freckles—now more prominent than before—dotted her soft cheeks.

Father Dyer got up and hugged her. Ringlets of black hair flooded his face—and he drew in the scents of coconut and vanilla. He held her tightly. The warmth of her body felt as good as he remembered.

16

"Look at you," she said.

He smiled. "How long's it been?"

"Forever," she said.

"Have a seat. Would you like some tea?"

"Sure," Beth said, smoothing out her skirt as she took the chair he offered.

Father Dyer plugged in his electric kettle, then sat back down. "Seriously, though, how long's it been? I can't believe you're here . . . just can't believe it."

"It'll be seven years in June."

"That long," he said. "Yes . . . I guess it has been. Are you back in Los Angeles?"

"I'm in Ojai, with my parents."

"I'll always remember those nights at your parents' house—the Sunday dinners, your dad's jazz music, your mom's meatloaf . . . shiny with ketchup. How are they?" Father Dyer said.

"Fine," Beth said.

They held each other's gaze for a few moments without speaking.

While Beth looked the same as ever, Father Dyer believed her to be different inside. Back then, she was always fast with a smile, but now she seemed distant, wearing an eyes-on-the-floor expression that suggested life had brought her responsibilities worthy of her age rather than an ability to cope with them.

"Is everything okay?" he asked.

"Yes, very good," she said. Beth stood up and walked around the office. She brushed Father Dyer's white Easter alb that hung on the back of his door and twirled her fingers around his matching stole. Her nail polish was Pentecost red, quite different from the French manicures she used to give herself as an undergrad. "It's so good to see you, Patrick, especially so . . . so in your element." She tucked a ringlet of hair behind her ear.

The kettle's water began to boil. Father Dyer perked up to the rumble, poured the scalding liquid into two mugs, and opened a flat wooden box containing assorted teas (a Christmas gift from a parishioner—he'd received four such boxes). Beth selected Earl Grey, while Father Dyer picked a raspberry blend. He preferred the former, but nobody ever chose fruit teas, so it fell to him to drink them. He lifted the bag in and out of his cup, allowing it to shed its red ribbons.

Beth blew across the surface of her tea.

"What have you been up to?" Father Dyer asked.

"Well," said Beth, playing with a turquoise ring on her index finger, "a lot's been going on, actually, but not all good."

"That's what we're used to in the church. No one comes here unless something's gone wrong. It's how we've survived for as long as we have. Other people's tough luck is our good fortune."

She drew a deep breath and cracked a polite smile. Father Dyer thought about apologizing for saying such a thing, but he knew her—she always had a good sense of humor, so he leaned back and sipped. He was used to spending time in the confessional, hearing these clipped statements, the foreshocks of trouble.

"My husband and I haven't been getting along. We, Mark and I, that is, have been arguing a lot the last few months . . . I won't bore you with such a thing, and then, about a month ago, he left."

"Oh, I didn't know you'd gotten married."

"Yes."

Father Dyer nodded.

"We married quick," Beth said, as if justifying it, "only a few months after you and me, actually."

18

"Oh, wow." Father Dyer took a sip and burned the roof of his mouth. "I didn't—"

"I thought of telling you."

"If you want, there's an excellent marriage counselor."

"It's just . . ." Beth said, taking another deep breath. "Patrick, do you remember that weekend we spent together, before you went to seminary?"

"Of course," Father Dyer said. He got up from his chair, went over to the door, opened it, and looked around—no one was there save for the image of Beth undressing in that dim New York hotel room, resting one hand on the nightstand while the other flipped off her heels. He envisioned her tan lines, heard her breath, felt her moisturized skin. Heat flushed his face, and his palms grew moist. He closed the door and returned to his desk.

"Anyway," Beth said, "that weekend, I got pregnant." Her voice dropped off at the end.

Father Dyer didn't answer. Shards of sunlight sliced through the window. He thought he'd escaped unscathed and been absolved of his sin through continuous commitment and prayer.

Beth continued: "I didn't tell you because you'd just gone to seminary, and then I met Mark. I let him think the baby was his. When Sam was born, Mark just thought he was premature. I never told him otherwise. You and Sam really look alike—floppy hair, thin lips, hazel eyes. There's—"

"Why are you telling me this now? What the hell am I supposed to do?" Blood beat in his ears, and his mouth went dry. He closed his eyes. "Why tell me?" he said softly.

"Nobody knows," Beth said.

"I know!"

"I'm . . ." Beth said. She pulled a tissue from her purse and dabbed her eyes. "I'm desperate, Patrick. Sam needs a man in his life, and I don't know a better one than you. He just hasn't been the same since Mark left. He doesn't draw or play anymore. He's just quiet . . . and too sad for a boy to be."

Father Dyer rested his head in his hands. He knew that, in time, Beth would get up and leave, but the problem wouldn't, and he'd replay that weekend in his head and wonder how he could have been so selfish. In the past, he'd justified it by saying to himself that it was before seminary, before he'd taken his vow. He even thought that it would make him a better priest, one that was *really* able to identify with carnal sin. Then he pictured his boy, Sam, crawling, standing, walking, and talking.

Beth uncrossed her legs and stood. "Goodbye, Patrick. I thought that maybe you'd . . . That's all, that maybe . . ." she said.

Father Dyer didn't budge, his eyes fixed on slats of hardwood. Beth draped her purse over her shoulder, slowly, as if she was allowing him time to get his thoughts together and possibly say something. When she realized he wasn't going to, she turned the brass knob and escaped down the hall, her high heels tapping the wood. He listened to her stride for as long as he could.

Minutes later, Father Dyer ran across the hall to the bathroom and threw up. He splashed some water on his face and inspected himself in the mirror. Cool beads of water slid over his skin, and he shut his eyes and listened to the hum of the air vent. For a minute or two, he tried not to breathe.

***

Later that evening, Father Dyer sat in the rectory watching his thirteen-inch black-and-white TV that he'd picked up at last month's rummage sale. While the buttons were worn, and the picture was a touch fuzzy, he liked how people looked in black and white better than in living color. He thought they seemed more noble and polished, rather than like real people undergoing real lives.

The Dodgers game was on, and in between pitches, batters, and innings, Father Dyer's mind wandered. He thought of Beth. In college, they'd both decided to study philosophy, and Patrick had often invited Beth to study with him. They'd grown close—Patrick's rigidity and Beth's blithe freedom an interesting mixture. He remembered her torn jeans, dreamcatcher earrings, laughing till his gut hurt, and her generous family. Thinking of her parents made him think of his. He remembered even as a boy discerning that they weren't right for one another. They were a cold couple with a big house, uncomfortable furniture, and shiny silverware—a house where laughter and smiles only escaped from the TV set. Only once did Father Dyer remember seeing his parents kiss; they'd probably kissed more often, but he was certain he'd seen it only one time: his junior year of high school, after he'd awakened in the hospital from a car accident. They'd stood together under the fluorescent lighting, the beep of the heart monitor in the background. Father Dyer had found his calling, but not as quickly as other priests, and while his love for the church was steadfast, his parents' life made him fearful of his ability to be a husband and father.

Even though Father Dyer had spent years burying the memories of that weekend with Beth, they breathed quite easily. He pictured the meal at the Italian restaurant where she'd ordered linguine with clams, the used bookstore where she'd scoured for collectible copies of anything André Gide, and the fancy boutiques where even window shopping seemed expensive.

That weekend, he'd made love to Beth four times. He recalled the smoothness of her calves, the saltiness of her neck, and the way she whispered his name with humid breath. After they were finished, she always placed her head on his chest and told him how strongly his heart beat. But as much as he cared for her, celibacy was a sacrifice he was willing to make to pursue his calling. He even felt exalted in having done so. Few knew that long ago, the church had allowed its priests to marry, but Father Dyer wholeheartedly supported the ways of the recent doctrine, believing that it was only possible to walk one path.

What he loved so much about the priesthood was that he couldn't hurt anyone. In front of the tabernacle, behind the altar, underneath the crucifix, in the sanctuary, life felt right. He was serving Him, and in a time where every Catholic story seemed to be less than savory news about priests and their hellish transgressions, he'd worked extra hard to restore the name of the church.

At St. John the Baptist Parish, Father Dyer was safe and respected. The way people looked at him was new and exciting, and while he reminded himself of Matthew's words, "Call no man Father," he was proud of what he'd become. He wasn't sure what would happen if St. John the Baptist Parish found out about his son; he figured that he'd be assigned to teach religion at the school. They'd place him as far in the background as possible—send him to raise funds and run bingo games. No longer would he stand on the steps. No longer would he lead Mass. He'd lose his pride and his calling.

He made himself an early dinner—a couple of scrambled eggs, a piece of dry toast, and a glass of water. He ate standing up over the sink, looking out the window, watching the clouds change positions and brighten and darken the day, sorry for the way he'd spoken to Beth. She'd been selfless, deceiving her son and husband and stuffing this secret for years so that he could live unburdened. It was hard to believe that he and Sam had lived separate lives under the same sky for so long. In the stillness, his mind continued to roam, and he didn't get in the way. What kinds of books does Sam like? he thought. Does he have many friends? Is he afraid of the dark? And then, Could I be a good father?

***

The pews were full. Easter Sunday brought in the "twice-a-yearers," as priests called them. Father Dyer stared over the paschal candles at the stained-glass window at the narthex of the church—a portrayal of Jesus, Mary, and Joseph. They looked peaceful, like the perfect nuclear family.

Father Dyer descended the steps and stood in front of the parishioners. "My friends," he said, "today, I'd like to talk to you about sacrifice. Jesus died for our sins. He gave His life. The ultimate sacrifice. I ask you—have we returned this sacrifice? Returned it to one another? If we wanted to repay His gift, we'd sacrifice more. We'd part with what is wanted and do what is right. There are many battles in Catholicism: right and wrong, sin and promise, receiving and giving, selfishness and sacrifice, death and resurrection."

Light poured through the Noah's ark stained-glass window on the gospel side of the church and tinted some of the parishioners' faces blue. Father Dyer dried a few beads of sweat from his upper lip with a handkerchief. A baby began to cry, and the baby's mother picked him up, headed toward the back, and bounced the kid's troubles away. Normally, Father Dyer tried his best to ignore crying babies, but now, the cry occupied his mind. It was easier to be a priest when he hadn't been so close to the life of a layperson.

"To me," Father Dyer said, "it's almost blasphemous to use the word *sacrifice* to describe what He did. That's because, in today's world, we've diluted the word's puissance. We use it to describe much less. Just the other day, I read in the paper that an athlete was *sacrificing* by deciding to take two million dollars less per year. Something that doesn't hurt you—hurt you seriously—that doesn't affect your life in a great way, is not *sacrifice*. Sure, it may be kind and generous, but it doesn't warrant being called *sacrifice*."

The mother with the crying boy continued to move back and forth, nuzzling and lifting the boy, pointing at the votive candles lined up before Mary. Father Dyer always liked the way the flames danced inside the red glass holders, and he often imagined for whom the wicks had been lit: a dying father, a couple in the midst of a rough divorce, an estranged husband, someone who needed the courage to sacrifice?

Father Dyer continued: "Many people ask me why the symbol of our church is a pelican. The pelican is the perfect representation of Jesus. I believe *vuln* is the word. When adult pelicans are unable to find food for their young, they vuln themselves, or rip flesh from their own bodies to feed their young. *That's* sacrifice," Father Dyer said, walking the polished floor. He felt warmed by the parishioners' gazes.

"I grew up going to church. Most of the children didn't like it—they doodled on the missal

24

envelopes and closed their eyes, like many of you are doing now . . . but I was always drawn to religion, uplifted, and I always dressed up. One day at Mass, a priest, Father McClintock, came up to me while I was tugging at my shirt and tie. He asked me if I was comfortable. 'No,' I said. 'Good,' he answered. The priest took a long look at me and said, 'Grace is never comfortable.' And I think the same thing of sacrifice. It's not effortless; it's not easy; it's *never* comfortable. Are there people out there that are deeply satisfied by such discomfort—I don't know. We need to try to be."

The congregation was quiet as Father Dyer took a long pause and let his words ring. "Remember Romans Twelve: Give Him your bodies as a living sacrifice, consecrated by Him, acceptable by Him. Prove in practice that the plan of God for you is good and move toward the goal of maturity."

After the sermon, Father Dyer walked to the altar and offered the blood and body of Christ: "This is my body, which will be given up for you." The altar boy rang the sanctus bells while Father Dyer placed the Host delicately atop his tongue and took a sip of sweet wine. He bowed his head. Usually, his prayers were short and crisp, but today they wobbled as he thought of Beth and Sam, and how he didn't want to go through life seeing children and knowing he'd abandoned his, and how he thought he'd be more needed as Sam's father than as God's servant.

When Mass concluded, Father Dyer exited the church and shook hands, greeted parishioners, and wished everyone a joyous Easter. Every so often, a gust of wind blew droplets from the church fountain onto Father Dyer's face.

"Thank you for a beautiful Mass," a woman said. Her lips were shiny, and a few curls spilled onto her forehead. She held a camera in her hand, and a man and two girls stood in front of the fountain, waiting for her to snap away.

"Would you like me to take the photo . . . so you can join in?" Father Dyer offered.

"Oh," she said, "I was just going to ask another parishioner."

"It's not a problem. I'm just like everybody else," he said, bringing his eye to the viewfinder and lining up the family of four. Father Dyer took his time, making sure the light was right and that there weren't any stray parishioners in the background, counted to three, and snapped the picture.

He continued to mingle, meet people from out of town, and thank families for coming.

Soon after, back in the rectory, he carefully removed his alb and put on his traditional black-and-white garb. He gazed out the window, sipping a glass of tap water, and watched family after family get in their cars and leave the lot. The once-loud sidewalk was quiet; only the wind stirred.

The sun was high, and Father Dyer stared directly at it. He closed his eyes and watched yellow dots float around the insides of his eyelids. Sam, he thought, was around seven years old, an age when, research had shown, the most important person in the family was the same-sex parent. It was his path: God had brought Beth to him; God needed him to be a father, to spend time with his boy, to live out the words of sacrifice he so proudly preached. After a few glasses of water, he walked out to the empty lot, got in his car, and drove off.

***

Traffic was fluid, and Father Dyer made good time. The ocean to his left, the dunes to his right. The windows were up, the radio off, and the cross that hung from the rearview mirror swayed. As the tires hummed on the asphalt, his mind drifted, and he thought of a Bible verse from Samuel: "Moreover, as for me, far be it from me to sin against the Lord by ceasing to pray for you, but I will instruct you in the good and right way." Verses regarding fatherhood came to his mind, too: "A father's responsibility is without question." "The father of one who is right with God will have much joy; he who has a wise son will be glad in him." "The righteous who walks in His integrity, blessed are his children after him."

A long time had passed since Father Dyer had been to Beth's parents' house in Ojai, but it was just as he remembered, with poppies blanketing soft hills, avocado trees standing in soldier-like rows, and the scent of rosemary and sweet dirt hanging in the air. Beth usually sat next to him, though, her window down, her right hand making aerodynamic shapes in the air. He turned down the gravel road without even needing to think about it. Pebbles crunched under his tires, and clouds of dust grew behind his car, just as they always had years before.

The two-story white rambler sat in the shade of a fortress of cypresses, a car and a truck in the driveway. He recalled the way Beth's dad always played Ellington records, and the way Beth's mother kissed him on both cheeks, as though she were French. He always sat across from Beth. He loved that whenever she smiled, she placed her tongue between her teeth, and he remembered that she always laughed at his bad jokes and told her own about Professor Neblett, the philosophy chair, and his watching-paint-dry class.

Father Dyer parked a little ways from the house and opened his window enough to let a breeze whisper across his forehead. He relished the sounds of the country: the chirp of a bird, the sigh of rustling leaves, and the hiss of industrial sprinklers.

A basketball hoop with a frayed net and worn backboard was nailed to an oak. He smiled when he thought of Sam shooting. A tree stump stood not far from the basket, and Father Dyer wondered whether Sam had ever attempted a shot while standing atop it.

He got out of his car, exhaled long and steady, and headed toward the home. The pickup in the driveway was cooling down and making little ticking noises.

The front door was a Dutch door with the top half open. Father Dyer wasn't sure whether he should knock or just call hello.

Just then, he heard a little boy's laugh coming from inside.

Father Dyer stood still, frightened, rehearsing "Hi Sam" over and over. The boy laughed again. His giggle sounded a lot like Beth's—high and lingering. A gentle burn spread in his limbs, and his chest welled with joy. He imagined his boy sitting on the floor and wearing a white T-shirt and navy shorts. Maybe a shoelace untied.

He kept quiet, trying his best to absorb Sam's voice. Did he detect the enthusiastic rubbing of pencil on paper?

"You're turning into Picasso over there," a man said. His voice was gravelly. "Let's see what you got." The man cracked open a can.

"One second," Sam said. Pencils dropped to the floor and rolled along the hardwood. "Okay, Dad, I'm ready."

Father Dyer's neck flared with bright pain.

"You'll be better on my lap," the man said, followed by a grunting sound and a "there we are."

28

"Remember that day at the beach?" Sam said. His voice was soft, and Father Dyer savored his words.

"Of course," the man said. "What a picnic."

On the wall opposite the door, atop a varnished table, was a photo: Beth, Sam, and presumably Mark. They were all wearing jean shirts and loud smiles.

"That's what I've been drawing," Sam said. "Look!" Paper crinkled and then Sam explained: "That's me, right there, with the striped shirt and basketball shoes. And there, that's Mom. She has on her high heels and sunglasses, and there, that's you, with the hat."

Father Dyer drew a deep breath and shut his eyes.

"I don't wear those kinds of hats," the man said. "I look like Lincoln!"

Sam giggled. "I know. I messed up and tried to fix it."

As Sam continued to talk about that day at the beach with seagulls, sand, and sun, Father Dyer peeled open his eyes and scanned the foyer. He stared at the smattering of photos, the vase full of tired gardenias, and a pile of different-sized shoes strewn next to the hallway closet. He swallowed hard and walked back to his car, stepping only where his feet wouldn't make any noise.

FOREST FOR THE TREES

"What's that?" Emily turned Kaleb's way and knocked a pillow to the floor. She said it again.

"Hmm?" Kaleb said, half-asleep.

"That noise," Emily said. She placed her hand on Kaleb's chest. "Do you hear that?"

Kaleb took a second, rubbed his eyes, and worked his tongue around his mouth. "It's just the wind, sweetie, or a raccoon. I've seen a lot of them lately." He opened one eye and took in what he could. Emily was sitting up in bed, both her hands in tight fists, craning her head back and forth. "Just relax, baby. Go back to sleep."

Even though it was only early November, winter had already arrived, announcing its presence last week with a snowstorm and consistent below-freezing temperatures. Just then, a gust swooped through the White Mountains and rattled the roof of their secluded cabin. The long-tongued draft agitated the remaining flames in the nearby Franklin stove, inducing a succession of machine-gun pops that startled them both. "You're right," Emily said, "maybe it *is* just the wind." She dropped back into the sheets.

A minute passed, and Kaleb tried to get comfortable. He tossed and turned and lined his gaze with the ceiling. Moonlight broke through a slit in the drapes, forming a white Rorschach-style blot on the ceiling that resembled an M16 rifle, the weapon he'd carried while serving in Afghanistan. "Go long!" A football spiraling across the sky. Sergeant Wiggins going deep. A land mine. Wiggins's femur poking through bloodied skin. Kaleb scooping him up, waving down a Humvee in the distance, feeling warm blood wash over his arms.

"Kaleb! Do you hear that?"

"What?"

"For Christ's sake—the noise, *that* noise."

Kaleb sat up and took a peek toward the doorway at the opposite end of the room. There was a figure there, its silhouette tall and strong, backlit by what little light the Franklin stove's embers had left to offer. Emily stared in the direction of the figure, most likely believing that everything was fine because Kaleb was still. When her eyes made sense of the person in the doorway, she didn't scream. She trembled. As the bed shook beneath him, Kaleb wedged himself tightly against Emily and wrapped his arm around her quivering stomach. He then reached for her hand, but her fingers were too rigid to be held.

"Don't move," the man said. His voice was deep and soft, hard to hear with the wind whirring outside. "No Superman shit. Just stay there. Both of you."

Stuttered breaths escaped Emily's mouth one after the other, and Kaleb's heartbeat sped up, switching from sleeping rhythm to a jogging-like clip. "Please," Kaleb finally said, "just don't hurt us. Take whatever you like. We don't have much. I'm a park ranger, and my wife's a painter. I—"

"Shut up." The man was still camouflaged by the darkness. He hadn't moved an inch. None of his features were visible.

Kaleb went on: "There's a shoebox. In the closet. With some cash in it. It's all yours. Please, don't hurt my wife. Don't hurt us."

The room was still. There were only Emily's trembling wheezes and the scraping of an animal on the roof, long claws ripping at the shingles.

"It's very simple," the man said. His voice was steady and monotone, softening at the end of each sentence, as if he was bored. "Do as I say. If you don't, I'll kill you both. First thing I want you to do is get out of bed and walk with me to the living room. Can you do that?"

Neither Emily nor Kaleb answered, so the man raised his voice and repeated the question.

"Yes," they both said in unison.

"Good."

Emily tugged on Kaleb's arm. She needed him. He'd managed to avoid capture during his six years of duty in the Middle East, but he knew plenty who hadn't, and the ones who'd made it out always said that the best thing to do was to make the aggressors feel as if they were in total control.

The man clicked on the hallway light, and Kaleb's and Emily's eyes adjusted to the brightness. They took him in. He was tall, wearing jeans and a navy hooded sweatshirt. He had a stocking cap pulled over his face, with holes cut out for his dark eyes and small mouth. "Pretty stupid of you," he said, pointing at Kaleb, "to put your gun cabinet by the entrance." He yanked a nickel-plated six-shooter—a pistol Kaleb had purchased a few weeks ago—from the waist of his jeans and pointed the barrel their way. He led them both into the living room where he clicked on another lamp. He licked his teeth and made them both sit on the couch.

Again, the fire popped, and cold wind pummeled the house. A green duffel bag lay on the floor, and the man pulled a tangle of rope from it. Kaleb straightened his spine, and the man pointed the gun at his head. "Whoa, what'd I say about being Superman?" The man looked in the direction of Kaleb's gaze and noticed two cell phones charging on a coffee table. He stepped backward, continuing to point the gun in their direction. When he finally reached the table, he turned and smashed both phones with the gun. He continued long after shards of glass screens and pieces of plastic were strewn about the carpet, just beating the table—metal on wood, a solid pounding that brought Kaleb back to the desert, with Wiggins screaming: "Don't let me die, Kaleb. Please don't let me die."

"Landline," the man whispered. "Your landline? Where is it?"

"Right there," Emily said. "Behind you. In the kitchen." She could barely get the words out, and when she did, her body convulsed.

The man backed up slowly, his gun pointed directly at them, alternating between their two bodies every few seconds. He clobbered the phone with the heel of the gun. Then he strolled back to Kaleb and Emily, humming a tune—a high note, then a low note.

First, he tied up Kaleb. A couple of times, Emily looked over at the man and even gazed at Kaleb, her eyes saying, "I'm sorry." Kaleb stayed still and allowed the man to finish up. His mouth had gone dry, and he did what he could to gather some moisture, going as far as to suck on the insides of his cheeks. After his hands and feet were tied up, the man moved on to Emily, first blindfolding her with a red bandana that was dirty with what looked like car grease, then poorly wrapping her wrists and ankles with rope. She incomprehensibly babbled in bursts, as if she were speaking in tongues, and the sounds lingered in Kaleb's ears. The only noise he'd ever heard that sounded similar was when he'd cornered a member of the Taliban in a house outside of Kabul. He remembered the repeated syllables that had spouted from the man's mouth: *jan-da jan-da jan-da.* He'd pulled the trigger, then turned to see a cloaked woman clutching a newborn.

When the man grabbed Emily by the arm and led her toward the back door, she gagged, and a torrent of vomit splattered on the carpet, bits of beets in brown puddles, like pieces of exploded flesh. She squirmed and did her best to pull away, but she was too puny, and once he pressed the barrel of the six-shooter against the back of her temple, she went soft, her knees weak, as if she hadn't any bones in her body, and he threw open the back sliding door and led her into the night.

Kaleb wrestled with the ropes. He tugged and yanked, spread his hands apart again and again, doing whatever he could to loosen the cords. Outside, Emily finally screamed for help. "Please," she begged. "Kaleb!" Cold blasts of wind struck Kaleb as he did his best to get to her, tumbling and rolling to the opened back door. From the carpet, he saw the man open the trunk of a car and shove Emily inside. Kaleb writhed on the floor and shouted, but no one would hear a thing with the brash wind and the nearest neighbor miles away. The man got into the driver's seat, closed the door, and headed up the long, snowy driveway to the main road.

Soon after the man's car had taken off, Kaleb was back in Army mindset. Adrenaline flushed his legs, and his chest tingled. He'd been back eight months, but he already pined for the rush of war, the desire to help, to fight, and to be needed by his fellow soldiers. More than anything, he missed being a hero. He craved the way Emily used to speak to him when he was a soldier. He had noticed that, these days, whenever he told people he worked as a park ranger at Jericho Mountain State Park, Emily was quick to say, "Yeah, he does that now. A little something for him to stay busy. But he used to be in the Army, fighting in Afghanistan." Most people thanked him for his service and never asked about the park job. Why would they? It was nothing more than babysitting trees. "And it bothers you, that she says that? That she always talks about your past?" The psychiatrist had continued muttering: "Are you sure you're okay? It's not your fault that Wiggins is dead. So you guys were throwing a football around. It's tough to come back. Trust me, I know. War is cocaine, and the rest of the world is decaf coffee. Kaleb?"

The man had done a lousy job tying Kaleb's hands together, using nothing other than bow knots that weren't effective for rope because the ends were too thick. In less than two minutes, Kaleb had worked his hands free and managed to crawl to the kitchen where he grabbed a bread knife and cut through the rope that fastened his feet. He sawed through in little time and was up, throwing on a coat and jeans, and grabbing his other firearm—a Glock—that he had stowed away in the pantry behind some canned goods. He slammed a magazine into the base, ripped his keys from the hook near the back door, and sprinted to his truck. She wasn't far. She couldn't be. The main road only went south a half mile, maybe less. The man had to have gone north.

He hopped in his truck, shoved the key into the ignition, and lit the motor. He took off, the tires spluttering on the soft ground, then catching and kicking up clumps of snow. Never again had he thought he'd feel the burn of war. It was a muscle, he'd thought, that would quickly atrophy, but here he was, and he could hear Wiggins rattle in his brain: "Attention, soldiers. A woman was taken from this cabin. Suspect heading north, driving a sedan with a broken taillight." He sped northward, his foot heavy on the gas and his hands tight on the steering wheel.

There was nothing in this New Hampshire night—just coldness and darkness and some flakes of snow. His radio played but was too soft to hear, and when he did pick up on it, he shut it off and delivered a few controlled puffs of air.

The shrink was right: coming home from war wasn't easy. Kaleb had thought it was probably a lot like getting out of jail. The real world and military life were different existences. He'd gotten used to writing Emily cards and having her send him packages stuffed with taffy and black licorice and Dunkin' Donuts coffee. He'd loved the way she wrote the *E* in *Emily*, curly and round, like a backward three, and that she'd always signed each card with "XOXO." Many times, he'd even pressed his lips to the seal of the envelope knowing her lips had been there first. She seemed to love him more when he was away. In every card she'd sent to base, she'd used the words *brave* and *hero*, and since he'd been back, she'd never called him those things. They'd only made love nine times, too, and he worried that she was no longer attracted to him without the uniform. He'd even caught her once, in the ricochet of the bathroom mirror, standing by his closet and brushing the fibers of his dress uniform.

As he navigated the switchbacks, he thought he could see a red dot in the distance. It was the red dot of one taillight, but it was quick to disappear as Kaleb careened into a sharp turn. The tires skittered as the heavy Ford leaned into the curve, but Kaleb pushed hard, trying his best to close the gap. His mouth had gone dry again, and his teeth had started chattering. The forest flanked both sides of the icy road, and Kaleb pictured men deep in the dark, painted with mud, lurking behind the pines and maples. *Jan-da jan-da jan-da. Jan-da jan-da.* A clicking sound popped into his head, too, the snapping of a rifle bolt, and he shifted his

37

weight on his seat, crinkling a page from last week's local newspaper. He'd been on patrol as usual at the state park; the Wednesday had been calm. No one had picnicked or camped, just a few hikers had passed through. Kaleb had read the paper in his booth and come across an article: "Lifeguard at YMCA Pool Saves Teenage Girl." He'd even managed to memorize a few of the sentences from the teenager: "I just couldn't catch my breath, and I started to panic and choke. It was horrible. It all went fast, and then he was there, and I was in his arms, and he brought me up, like an angel, like a hero." After Kaleb had finished the article in his booth, his cell phone rang. He'd picked up, and the woman on the other end of the line had detailed that there was a man in the woman's restroom by White Birch Trail. "I think he's high," she'd said. "Maybe heroin. I definitely saw a needle. That's heroin, right? The one with the needle?"

The speedometer pointed at fifty. Again, Kaleb felt his truck plane, so he let his foot off the gas and drove in the center of the road, where his knobby Goodyears straddled the yellow dividing lines. Was Emily still crying for him? Where did she think she was going? Did she know that he was coming after her? He played her cry in his mind and heard the way she held onto the *a* in *Kaleb.* Her voice was fragile, like a little girl's, helpless and pure. He'd never seen her like that, and he never wanted to again.

Snow fell harder and faster now, and Kaleb flipped on his wipers and watched the powder smudge across the windshield. He cranked the defroster to max. He was closing in on the man. "And how long have you heard the voices? The screams? What are those words? Are they Arabic or something? And you've been counting heads in restaurants, grocery stores, and shopping malls? All the time? Do you own any guns? Kaleb? Do you hear me, Kaleb?"

He slapped his face and shook his head. The Glock dug farther into his stomach, and he readjusted it. Kaleb always believed that heroism was less about bravery and more about timing. The ability to show courage wasn't rare; the opportunity was. He concentrated on the man's single taillight, a glowing spot of red, a setting sun. "Emily!" he called out. "Emily!"

The road climbed. A gust kicked up, too, causing a swirl of flurries to brush against the truck. Kaleb smashed the gas pedal and gripped the wheel harder. He was almost there now, no more than a quarter mile away. His thoughts turned back to that day last week: After the woman had called him, he'd gone to the restroom. It wasn't uncommon for junkies to seek refuge in the park, and he'd been hard on them, hoping that if word spread, they'd stop coming. As soon as Kaleb had pushed open the bathroom door, the stench of urine had made him cringe. Day had broken through the plastic skylight in the ceiling and lit a man who was wedged between the sink and the trashcan. The man had worn olive cargo pants and a white stained T-shirt that was stretched over a muscular torso. A jacket was tucked behind his head, and his sleepy eyes roamed the restroom. Even though it was chilly out, the man had been sweating, and his cheeks were ruddy.

"Emily!" Kaleb screamed as the shafts of his headlights finally lit the bumper of the man's car. He checked his Glock, made sure it was still tucked into his jeans, and chewed on the inside of his cheek till he drew blood. "I'm coming for you," he whispered. If he managed to save her, what would the paper read? Would the headline mention the word *hero*, like the article he'd put to memory? Could Emily hear the growl of his engine? Often when he arrived home from work, she'd say, "Knew you were home. Heard your truck from far away." He accelerated, hoping the rumble of his hearty V-8 would reach her ears.

The road now descended. Kaleb let his foot off the gas and watched the RPM needle slide down to two thousand. He neared the old sedan, was no more than twenty feet away now, his brights shining through the back window. And then, just after mile-marker thirty-nine, without slowing down, the man swung his car off the main road onto a dirt path. Kaleb hammered the brakes, and the Thermos that rested on the passenger seat pinged off the dash and rolled around on the floor. Kaleb didn't follow. He stayed straight on the main road. He knew this area far better than the man. He knew it far better than anyone, actually. Day after day, he had surveyed this outer fringe of the park, even made himself get lost just to find his way out. The man had just turned off onto an emergency fire trail that led to a large clearing in the forest. Let him think he pulled one over on me, Kaleb thought, knowing that there was another entrance to the very same clearing at mile-marker forty. From forty, it was actually a smoother drive to the clearing, too, so with his 4x4, he was certain he'd beat the man to the spot.

In the quiet of the truck's cabin, he remembered the desperation in the druggie's voice: "Please," he'd begged, "don't call the police. Don't make me go back to jail! I can't! My wife and kids. Just . . . please! I beg of you! I'll do ten years this time." The man had collapsed onto the floor, the words having drained him. His chest had risen and fallen rapidly. A syringe had dropped from his left hand and rolled toward Kaleb's boots. Kaleb hadn't said a thing.

40

He'd grabbed his phone from his pocket and dialed the police.

His headlights grazed the green mile-marker forty sign. He tapped the brakes and swerved onto the trail. His palms were sore from clutching the wheel so tightly, and he removed them after completing the turn and opened and closed his hands to get some of the feeling back. He started down the trail. He could hear Wiggins again, dishing out details, telling him where to be and what to do and how to get in and get out, and he started to visualize the scenario, even see Emily's face when he took control. She'd beam. She'd know she made the right decision to marry him, and she'd be overjoyed that her soldier was back home and all hers. She'd no longer have to tell her friends about his past in order to validate his present. No, the papers and the local—maybe even the national—news shows would do that for her. Even the other rangers who'd been on the job longer and who had more seniority would be intimidated. Maybe they wouldn't try to push weekend duty on him any longer. Maybe Emily would leave her painting studio to come on a hike with him, and they'd finally get around to having a family, as they'd so often talked about in their letters. "I'm glad your wife sent you to me, Kaleb. She loves you so much. There are medications that may help. Many people in your position are like powder kegs. You're courageous to come here. You're courageous to your core."

When he began the decline into the clearing, he canvassed the surroundings. It was a straight shot. He then killed the headlights, shut off the engine, and coasted down the trail in neutral. There were no other lights on the scene yet, and Kaleb gathered that he'd beaten the man to the clearing. Wind traced the truck and, without the engine running, the cabin turned cold

41

fast. Kaleb's eyes were dry. He blinked a few times to get some of the moisture back. He'd save his Emily. He knew he would.

He hit the brakes and clicked on the lights one last time. Then shut them off for good. He was about halfway down the incline, less than a hundred yards from the clearing. He yanked the emergency brake and popped out of the truck. He didn't want to be in the actual clearing when the man arrived with Emily. He wanted to take the man by surprise. The weather had dropped even more, into the high twenties, and the snow had made the ground wet and slushy.

Deep in the timber, there was a thickness to the quiet—dark and rich. Only the sounds of his body against the night. One step, then another. He heard his heart, his grinding teeth, and a steady ringing in his ears. This was just like the days in the mountains near Kandahar. He always heard this faint drilling sound in his ears when he was focused. It was his brain's way of letting him know he was ready. He took deep breath after deep breath and tried to get his fingers to stop twitching. Crouching, he pressed on toward the clearing, stepping over fallen branches and stray pinecones, amazed at how well he navigated without the weight of body armor. Were people behind him? Following him? Scurrying, laughing? He even thought he could hear Wiggins snickering and the cloaked woman and her baby crying. They seemed close, right around the corner. *Jan-da jan-da jan-da.* He ripped his Glock from his jeans and swung the gun around. "Leave me alone," he whispered.

Columns of light sliced through the forest from the northern end of the clearing, and then Kaleb heard the sounds of tires crunching snow and gripping against rough road. He took cover behind a pine. The wind kicked up again, blasting Kaleb, making him turn his back and wait until the gale had passed. He continued, wending through the forest, ripping through thickets of shrubbery and messes of undergrowth and swamps of mud that tugged at his boots and pant legs. His teeth knocked together, and the ringing in his ears grew sharper.

He could now make out the man's running car. He gripped his Glock tighter. The cold, military-grade plastic felt right against his palm as he brought the barrel in the direction of the man's vehicle. He was only twenty yards out now.

As he neared the clearing, Kaleb tried to inspect the man. It was black everywhere but where the headlights lit, and the man couldn't be spotted. He gathered the man was at the trunk when he heard the latch unlock, the hinges squeak, and Emily scream. The scream didn't even sound human, and in this open air, it carried like a wave and pinged in Kaleb's ears for several seconds. He wanted to call out: "Emily, I'm here. I'm here for you. I love you. Please don't leave me." He tucked his gun back into his jeans and blew on his hands.

The man grabbed Emily and took her out in front of his car. The headlights were bright and beaming and lit the cold forest perfectly. He shoved her, and because her feet were tied, she tumbled face-first to the ground, causing the red bandana to loosen and fall to her side. Traces of powder rose into the shafts of the car's lights. The man stood in front of the car, pointed the gun at her, and told her in a steady voice, "Don't try anything."

Kaleb swallowed hard and tasted some blood from his chewed cheeks. It had always helped him to count down when he was this focused, and so he did. He positioned himself on the ground, propped his elbows, pointed the Glock, took aim at the man's chest, and waited for him to stabilize. *Jan-da jan-da jan-da*. He started counting down from ten. Nine. Emily lay motionless on the ground, her face angled in Kaleb's direction. Eight. Her eyes seem to speak to him. Big and clear, begging for help. Seven. Six. And then she screamed again, pleaded. Five. Her eyes snapped shut. "Kaleb!" she said. Four. "Please! Kaleb!" In possibly her last breaths, it was his face and name that came to her so easily. Even in this cold, Kaleb felt his neck and face grow hot. Three. Kaleb exhaled. Two. One.

The gun jumped in his hands.

A shell sputtered from the magazine.

A single shot from the dark forest.

He'd hit the man in his left shoulder. Then he fired three more times. Blood and brain matter erupted from the man's head as the fatal bullets struck. The man's legs buckled, and his body went down in a heap, his head smacking the front bumper of his car as he fell. Once on the ground, his legs jerked, and his hands clawed at the snow. That was number thirty-three. At this point it was easy, routine. Kaleb was used to the smell of sulfur, the sound, the power of the trigger, and he let out a breath he'd been holding and pushed himself off the ground. He tucked his Glock into his coat pocket, against his heart.

Emily shrieked and twisted her head from side to side. Gasps left her mouth fast and hard, and strands of hair fell in front of her eyes as she searched the surroundings. "Help!" she managed to say, and Kaleb stepped out of the forest and into the clearing and rushed her way.

"Emily," he said. He entered the light, dropped down, brushed the hair from her face, and watched her eyes widen. She gazed at him the way he'd always wanted her to—with awe. She cried as he pulled a pocketknife from his jeans and cut through the loose

44

rope that wrapped her hands and feet. He pulled her up, and she gripped his back and shoulders. Her words were hurried and soft, but he made out, "Saved me." And she was right. He had. Now she had proof. All of it hadn't happened overseas, in another land, but here in her zip code, where she was born and raised. "I love," she said. "I love." And he dug his hands into her hair and pulled the thin fabric of her pajamas. "Me too," he said.

Behind Kaleb and Emily, the man groaned one final time. The sound reminded Kaleb of when he'd first seen the man in the women's restroom, high on heroin. "Please, man!" he'd begged. "I'll do whatever you want. *Whatever*!" And Kaleb had stopped dialing, the article still very much on his mind: "I just couldn't catch my breath, and I started to panic and choke. It was horrible. It all went fast, and then he was there, and I was in his arms, and he brought me up, like an angel, like a hero." Kaleb had invited the man into his truck, gotten all of his information. "I'll let you go, never mention this to anybody, under one condition. That you do something for me." And Kaleb had gone on, detailed the plan, told him that the back door didn't lock, told him about the gun cabinet, told him about the phones, and told him not to tie him up too good. "Keep yourself straight till then, too," Kaleb had said. "Afterward, get as high as you want. All right? Got it?" The man had nodded. "Mile-marker thirty-nine?" the man had repeated. "And you'll enter at forty. Once I'm there, get her out of the car, walk her to the front. And you'll just shoot a warning shot high above my head, scare me off, and I'll get back in my car. That will be it? You'll just let it all go? Blow over?" Kaleb had nodded, a smile forming on his face. "Exactly," Kaleb had said. "Now say it all again."

A swirl of wind overtook the clearing, powering against bark, and scattering flurries. Emily and Kaleb huddled together in the bright light. Emily's body convulsed, and she sobbed and clawed at Kaleb's back. Even through his thick jacket, he could feel her nails on his spine, and it reminded him of the way they used to love one another, before he'd enlisted. She squeezed him hard, as if she'd never let go, then tighter, until he found it difficult to breathe.

The gun popped in his breast pocket.

Emily jumped back, and Kaleb coughed and tried to catch his breath. It took him a moment to realize what had happened. In his excitement, he hadn't clicked on the safety. Emily was frozen, her mouth open, and they locked eyes as Kaleb brought the zipper down on his jacket, revealing a red circle on his T-shirt that grew by the second. She hurried over and yanked his shirt up. One bullet right in the abdomen. He hadn't felt anything, actually. He coughed more and started to choke on his own blood. Then his legs went numb, and he fell back on the ground and aligned his gaze with the tops of trees and the yellow tendrils of light that illuminated the many flakes.

The sharp, clean evergreen scent of the forest and the soothing wetness of the snow—it all came through so easily. He pictured the football spiraling through the hot air and dropping perfectly into Wiggins's arms. Then Wiggins was laughing and doing a celebratory dance. Kaleb's eyes stayed open, and Emily hovered above him. Once more, he pulled a labored breath through his mouth and felt his warm blood coat his stomach and chest. "No," he heard Emily say over and over again. "No." She placed her hands about his body, but the blood continued to seep, saturate her pajamas, run over his flesh, and pool on the white ground. She gazed at him with her large eyes, her pupils stretched to the rims of her brown irises—the same ones that had beckoned him to kiss her that night on the Hampton Beach boardwalk right after the movie on their way to the diner to share gravy-soaked fries. He saw the two of them, under soft streetlights, strolling to the front door, her hair dancing with the salty breeze, his hand attached to hers, and then he heard her whisper fade through the walls of his consciousness: "Hero. Hero. My hero."

PARTY OF TWO

Herbert and Marilyn walked into the newest diner in town, the Brown Bag. A yellow GRAND OPENING banner hung the length of the wall behind the hostess stand, and a greasy smell of overdone french fries lingered in the air. Herbert trudged to the front and put his name on the list. The hostess said it would be a few minutes. He headed back to the door and plopped down on a bench next to Marilyn.

"Few minutes," he said. "It's always a few minutes. Do you have that coupon?"

Marilyn unzipped her purse and spotted the piece of newspaper torn from the *Los Angeles Times*. On it was an illustration of a Dagwood sandwich piled high. The sandwich had cartoon eyes and thin arms and legs; it even sported basketball sneakers. None of it made Marilyn particularly hungry. What did LA people know about delis? Why were people always trying to be something they weren't? And why was Herbert so cheap? He'd made all this money as a CPA, and here they were only going out to eat because of a coupon. "Yes," she said. "It's here."

Whenever they went out, she realized just how estranged they were. At home, there were so many distractions: she knitted and read her romance novels, and he gardened and worked on an old Moto Guzzi in the garage. They bumped into one another in the hallway and, like coworkers, were always polite.

A waiter dropped a tray of dishes. White plates and tall glasses exploded on the black-and-white tiles. The waiter's face flushed, but as soon as the clientele applauded, his redness evaporated.

The door swung open, and a young man and woman entered. They were holding hands and couldn't have been more than twenty. The man looked a lot like Major, Marilyn's first boyfriend, and the girl didn't look like anyone Marilyn knew, but she looked cute with her sundress and strappy shoes. It wasn't sundress or strappy-shoes weather, but sometimes a woman had to make it the kind of day she wanted.

The young man really did look like Major, though, with a few twenty-first-century adjustments: his hair was longer and lighter, and his clothes were too big for his frame. His wallet had a chrome chain that connected from one of his belt loops to his back pocket, and he hadn't shaved in a few days. She never saw Major unshaven. The man had the same dark eyes and subtle freckles on his cheeks. He caught Marilyn staring at him. She smiled. He did the same. Soon after, the young woman went over and put her name down on the list. When she returned to the man's side, they shared a secret and then a kiss. A peck on the cheek transformed into a soft-lipped kiss, and before Marilyn knew it, the young man's and woman's lips had opened and were pulling on each other's. They shut their eyes, and the man moved one of his hands to the woman's neck. Herbert looked away. The couple stopped. The woman giggled and wiped her lips with the palm of her hand.

"Didn't know this was a goddamn brothel," Herbert said under his breath.

"Herbert! For two!" the hostess called.

Herbert and Marilyn followed the hostess and navigated their way from table to table, even one where some of the waitstaff had assembled and were belting out "Happy Birthday" to a little girl with pigtails. Marilyn blew the girl a kiss.

The hostess showed them to a red vinyl booth.

"Do you have a table?" Herbert asked. "I just can't stand booths. Always too far from the table."

The hostess scanned the restaurant and tucked a pencil into her bun. "No, none available right now, but I can put you back on the list and let you know when something opens up."

"That's all right," Herbert said. "I'm hungry." He slid into the booth.

"My grandpa hates booths, too," the hostess said. "Enjoy." She headed away from the table and back to her station.

"Always someone's grandpa these days," Herbert said.

"What do you expect? We're old," Marilyn said.

"Kids are too honest. That's all. Back in my day, we said what was polite, not what was true."

"Where are the menus?"

"Doesn't matter. We're just getting what's offered on the coupon."

"I wonder if they have sweet potato fries. I read that they're actually kind of good for you."

"Where the hell's the waitress?"

The affectionate couple was shown to the booth opposite Herbert and Marilyn. They plopped onto the same side of the booth, slid to the far end, and pressed right up against each other. They overlooked the busy street. The woman tucked some hair behind her ear and kissed the man's cheek. The man's neck sported a lipstick imprint, a perfect circle of red. They had menus in front of them but didn't seem interested. They studied the traffic and passersby, and the young woman muttered something about a crow—something about how it was the only bird without a song.

What if Herbert had gone to architecture school as he'd wanted when they'd first met? Would he

51

have been happier and, thus, made her happier? What if she hadn't gotten pregnant right away with the twins, forcing him to marry and stick it out at his father's accounting firm? Did he blame her for all of that?

She shifted her gaze to the young man. How she missed Major. He was her first love. They had both grown up on the same street in Montpelier, Vermont. They had gone to the same grammar school, middle school, and high school. Always close and friendly, they became closer one night. It happened a week or so into their tenth-grade summer vacation. Major's family had thrown a party for his older brother who'd recently graduated college. Marilyn had been happy as she danced in a dress that, she thought, looked similar to the young woman's. She had been a bit tipsy with champagne and had spotted Major outside in a field of tall grass. It had been late, but still light out. Major had walked toward her and asked whether she wanted to go for a stroll, head down to the Winooski River for a bit.

"Unbelievable," Herbert said. "No water. No waitress. Tell you one thing—they keep this up, they won't be busy for long."

"They just haven't got the kinks worked out yet."

"Some things never get the kinks worked out."

Marilyn nodded, pulled a napkin from the dispenser, and spread it across her lap. Again, she glanced at the couple. Her mind turned to Major. Down at the river, the two of them had dipped their feet into the Winooski, skipped stones, found stray branches, tossed them into the current and wondered where they'd end up. He'd kissed her—her first kiss— and she'd let herself go. She hadn't been sure how to kiss and had practiced on her bathroom mirror, but the real thing was different. She had left her lips parted and had let him do the work. Soft sounds had escaped her mouth, and the warmth of his touch had made her heart race.

"Where's the waitress?" Herbert asked the hostess as she rushed by.

"No one came by yet?" she said.

"Nope."

"Oh, wow. Opening weekend, you know?" She hurried off.

"What's with the 'opening weekend' stuff?" Herbert said. "It's a good thing these people don't make cars. Can you imagine? Oh, yes, the brakes didn't work. Sorry, sir. Brand new car—you know how it is?"

A laugh fluttered from the young couple's table. They kissed again. The man put his hand on the nape of the woman's neck, and Marilyn studied the way the woman's chandelier earrings swayed.

The waitress showed up and apologized. She was short with long bangs and puffy cheeks. "Everyone's got tons of coupons, and I didn't think this was my section. Wild, right?"

"I've heard wilder," Herbert said.

Marilyn pulled out the coupon and slid it across the table.

"To drink?" the waitress asked.

"A water for me," Herbert said.

"And I'll take a vanilla shake."

"You got it. Thank you," the waitress said. She spun around and took the young couple's order. They no longer kissed. They ordered something called "The King and Queen Platter." The man looked exactly like Major when he laughed—the way he snapped his head back and then covered his mouth with his right hand, as if he never wanted to chuckle in the first place. After that night, she and Major had gone steady. Two years later, he was drafted for Vietnam. The night before he deployed, she'd met up with him at the Winooski, only a stone's throw from where they'd first kissed. "I'll be back soon. We'll meet here again. I promise," he'd said. Marilyn had cried, then said, "I wish your parents hadn't named you Major. You can't expect not to be drafted with a name like that."

"They're back at it," Herbert said. "Will you look at these two kids . . . just kissing and kissing."

"It's . . . Isn't it just—"

"Exactly. It's just gross."

Marilyn took a deep breath. On October 12, 1972, Marilyn had driven with her family and Major's family to pick him up from the Burlington Airport. He'd strutted across the tarmac in a dark-green suit with gold buttons. He'd lost some weight, and his skin was tanned. He'd hugged her hard, till her back was sore. After a few hours together, Marilyn had headed off to work. "Tonight?" he'd asked. "Ten o'clock at the Winooski?"

Marilyn and Herbert's best day together had to be their wedding: big-band music, tiered cake, and a tossed bouquet. Since that time, it was as if someone had taken a quarter from their savings account each day. It was hard to notice the loss at first, but now, only a few wrinkled bills remained. She was glad her children had moved away, hadn't settled, and had searched for more.

"Miss!" Herbert called. "Miss!" The hostess scurried over. Herbert leaned her way. "Would you tell that couple to quit kissing. It's just not appropriate."

"Herbert," Marilyn said in a whisper.

The hostess craned her neck. The couple's bodies were intertwined: her hands in his hair, his fingers on her collarbone, their lips wrapped around one another's. Marilyn took in the other guests of the

54

restaurant. None of them seem to notice or care. Some ate; others laughed and wiped their ketchup-covered mouths.

"I'll get the manager," the hostess said.

"You can't tell 'em?" Herbert asked.

She headed off.

"Can you believe this?" Herbert said.

"Why?" Marilyn said. "What happened—"

"*What happened* is right. What happened to people, to manners, to all of it?"

A short time later, the manager, a tall bald man with dark circles under his eyes, delivered Marilyn's vanilla shake and Herbert's water. "What seems to be the problem?"

"Not *seems*," Herbert said. "What *is* the problem?" He pointed the way of the young couple.

"Oh. Okay, sure." The manager turned and took a few steps in their direction. He knocked on the far end of the table. The affectionate couple looked up. Their faces were rosy and their eyes large. "Please," he said. "It's makin' people uncomfortable."

Marilyn plucked a straw from the dispenser and dropped it into her shake.

"Uncomfortable?" the young woman said. "How? Why?"

"Are you kidding?" the young man said. "Just pathetic."

The manager's heavy footsteps softened as he headed away from the table. Herbert popped a baby aspirin in his mouth and downed it with a slug of water. Marilyn positioned her lips around the straw and drew in some vanilla milkshake. The cold drink soothed.

For the sake of her children and not wanting to be like her mother, Marilyn was demure, sweet, and always let Herbert get his way. She blamed herself; it could have been different if she'd just confronted him from time to time.

Laughter from the young couple wafted her way, and she thought of Major. Just as promised, he'd showed that night at ten at their usual spot on the Winooski, not far from the bridge. Even though it was October, the weather had still been tinged with summer. They'd kissed and talked but mostly held one another. "I'm going for a swim," Major had said. "Haven't been in this sweet river in too long. When I get out, I need to ask you something." He'd darted over to the bridge and stripped down to his boxers, then had brought his hands together above his head, bent his knees, and sprung forward.

Out of her periphery, Marilyn glanced the couple's way. They were playing a sort of game. She listened closely, straining her ears. "The sixth man to walk through the door," the young woman said. "That's what you're going to look like in fifty years. Wait for it, wait for it. Three, and there's four. And there's . . . there's! That's five. Come on, six! Lucky six!" They laughed. "The door stopped . . . What the . . . No, wait . . . Here it comes!"

She giggled, and the young man slapped the table.

"That's not even a man!" he said, laughing. "She's, like, twelve."

"Can't fight the game," she said.

Marilyn drank some more shake, then blotted her mouth with her napkin. She wondered about the young couple: where they'd met, how they'd met, whether it was love at first sight, or whether one of them really had to work for it. She always loved a good love story: Romeo and Juliet, Mark Antony and Cleopatra, even Lancelot and Guinevere.

The din of the diner was now percussive with the clamor of plates and flatware, laughter and conversation. A car in the parking lot revved its engine.

"Christ Almighty," Herbert said, throwing a glower the couple's way.

As Marilyn scanned the couple, the young man pulled his head back, opened his eyes, and drew in his partner. He smiled. Marilyn saw Major. She had witnessed him leap from the bridge, arc toward the water, and splash into the river. She'd clapped and smiled, her cheeks warm, and waited for him to pop back up. She'd wondered what his question would be. He hadn't yet come to the surface, and she'd called out and then yelled, screaming his name over and over, crying, "Major," so much and so hard that her throat burned. She'd sprinted into the water, her dress floating up around her. She'd waded out. She'd tried to find footing: "Major! Major! Major!"

The waitress swung by with a tray perched on her shoulder. She set it down on the edge of the table and placed a Reuben in front of both Marilyn and Herbert. "Can I get you guys anything else?"

"Tell those two to get a room," Herbert said.

The waitress took a glance. "Yikes! You bet." As she passed the young couple, she leaned forward. "Sorry, guys. Can't do that here. This is a family place, all right?" She pressed on, weaving her way to the kitchen doors.

Herbert took a bite and ran his tongue over his lips. Marilyn added a squirt of ketchup to her sandwich. She heard the young couple: "A family place?" the young man said. "How the hell do they think families are made?"

The young woman laughed. "Who the hell keeps snitching?" she asked. "No one in here seems to care except the damn waiters."

The young man cleared his throat. "It's him," Marilyn thought she heard the young man say. "The old man. I think it's him."

Major diving from the bridge burned brightly in her mind. They'd found his body the next day at dawn, a few miles down the river. She'd never loved a man as she'd loved Major. He was Paris, and everyone else was Cleveland. After him, she'd not wanted to be alone. A few months later, after she'd started at the barber college in upstate New York, she'd met Herbert. He was already frugal then, but he was tall and professional and he liked her. She knew that she'd be taken care of. She knew she'd no longer be alone. She knew they'd learn to live with one another, but never, like she and Major, *for* one another.

In fifty years, would the young woman look back and wonder about this guy, or would she be with him? Would they take trips from LA? Would they visit the Grand Canyon or see a show or two in Vegas? Would they still sit on the same side of the booth?

The diner's volume increased—a child at a nearby table began to cry, the restaurant's phone rang, a patron dropped some change onto the tile floor, and a car alarm blasted from the parking lot.

Marilyn swung her eyes to the right. The young couple was kissing. Their food had arrived, too, but it was just sitting there: a large platter piled with hamburgers, fries, onion rings, and two tall chocolate shakes with the leftovers in frosty metal tins, and strangely, two plastic crowns. One was fit for a king, the other a tiara. And then she remembered: the "King and Queen Platter."

She took another bite of her sandwich. The salty beef paired well with the creaminess of the shake, and she let the juices of both coat her mouth. The young couple took a break from kissing, placed the crowns on their heads, and resumed making out. This time, their kisses were wet and hard, and when the diner's noise softened, Marilyn heard their lips smack.

"For the love of God!" Herbert yelled in the direction of the young couple. He pounded his fists on the table, and the forks and knives jumped. "It's enough. We've been polite. But it's enough! It's like we're at some goddamn peep show."

The couple stopped kissing.

"Peep show?" the young woman said, then laughed.

Marilyn felt her hands grow warm and her lips quiver. She clenched her jaw and took her milkshake in her hands. Her stomach turned. She took a breath and felt Major's hands dig into her shoulder blades on the tarmac. She pictured the two of them on the riverbank, laughing, the flash of lightning bugs all around them.

The young man stared at Herbert. Marilyn swallowed. Her gulp felt so large that she believed everyone in the restaurant had seen it.

"What's your problem?" the young man asked. His voice was sharp. He wasn't afraid of Herbert. "We're two people in love. We're kissing. I haven't seen her in a while, and now I'm back, and I want to kiss my girlfriend."

"This is not the place. This is a restaurant." Herbert took a sip of water.

Little by little, a hush took hold of the place, and the attention of the diner turned the way of Herbert and the young couple. The crying baby didn't stop and neither did the phone or the commotion in the kitchen, but casual conversations were muted, laughter

59

paused, and bodies tensed. Even though Marilyn couldn't see all the people around her, she felt their eyes, their stares, and their focused burn.

"Haven't you ever been in love?" the young man asked.

"Of course," Herbert said. "That's not the point."

"That *is* the point," the man said. "You're a tired old man. There's nothing weird about two people who love each other kissing. It's about as interesting as a thirsty man drinking."

"It's not something that's done in public," Herbert said.

"Or, in your case, in private," the young woman added. "Look at her." The young woman pointed a finger Marilyn's way. "Does she look happy? When was the last time you kissed her?"

The manager hurried over. He stood between the two tables. He extended his arms in both directions. "Please, please. I need to ask you all to lower your voices. Either finish your meals quietly or leave."

The young man adjusted his crown, pulled a kosher dill from his plate, and gnawed off a hunk. "We're not going anywhere," the young man said.

"No service until it's too late! How many times did I ask you all to handle this situation? And what did you do?" Herbert's voice quivered.

"Situation?" the young woman said.

"I'm leaving. Let's go, Marilyn," Herbert said. "Come on. Let's get out of here." He slid to the edge of the booth and used the table to yank himself up.

Marilyn reached for her purse and began to scoot toward the aisle. Then she stopped. Her legs were weak and her body hot. She could feel the patrons inspecting her every move. She couldn't budge. She

60

didn't think she could even make it to the front door. "No," she said.

"Marilyn, come on," Herbert said. He walked her way as if to help her from the booth.

She pivoted her head and took in the clientele. They were fixated on her. Some chewed; others held fries and onion rings but were too captivated to put them in their mouths. "No," she said again. "I want to finish my sandwich. I want to stay here."

Again, Herbert reached for her arm, but she scooted back into the booth and picked up her Reuben. Herbert stormed away from the table and toward the front door, and she watched it swing open and fall back flush with the wall. She stared at him for as long as she could through one of the diner's windows, until his body was just a blotch in the parking lot.

With each bite, the racket grew, and when Marilyn was done with most of her sandwich, she peered the couple's way. They weren't kissing as before, but the woman had nestled her head alongside her man's.

Marilyn took a slurp of her shake. The young man smiled Marilyn's way, and she felt a grin form on her face. She loved the way his plastic crown sparkled in the afternoon sun. She kept stealing glances while taking bites, and every so often, she would close her eyes and hear the rush of the Winooski.

QUICKENINGS

1

At seventeen weeks, Larissa can feel her baby kick.
Sharing food and water, flesh and blood has bonded
her with her boy. With every ounce of added weight
and new curve appearing on the ultrasound, the more
aware she becomes of the world around him. She wants
society to be perfect, and even though it never will be,
there are still some things she can control.

2

Mr. and Mrs. Chaffey were generous people. They
called Larissa daily, fetched her groceries, and one
time, even bought her new pillows and a water filter.
"Anything for you," Mrs. Chaffey always said. But as
weeks turned into months and months became
trimesters, Larissa's premonition returned. The orange
chrysanthemums she'd gifted them had started it all.
Whenever she entered the Chaffeys' home, she noticed
the flowers on the tabletop, their petals drying and
resting at the base of the pot. Why was it not being
watered?

It upset her, but she tried to move forward. Her
intuition *was* her greatest gift, though one—much like
her cheekbones—that she'd done little to deserve. One
time, she changed meeting spots with a friend because
she had an inkling of fear, and something *did* happen: a
kitchen fire had overtaken the entire restaurant, killing
one. She'd also had a premonition with a well-
renowned photographer on a shoot in Brooklyn, and
later, after the ad was shot, he'd invited her up for
drinks, pinned her wrists above her head, and tried to
kiss her. She'd managed to free herself by sinking her

teeth into his right ear, then had hurried down the fire escape.

3

She enters the waiting area, plops in a seat, and squeezes her duffel between her sneakers. She only has the one bag, stuffed with a week's worth of clothes and a bunch of hotel-sized toiletries. It's not much to show for two-plus years in America, but she's had to act fast. Modeling happened in spurts—a gig here and there— but the world of go-sees and catwalks and cigarettes for dinner was never her thing, so she found work as a nanny. But when Caio, her brother, got sick, she needed more money, and a friend told her about the Chaffeys.

4

Just a simple transaction, Larissa told herself. She read over the Chaffeys' contract, even had her friend whose English was superior comb over the thick paragraphs. I can do it, she thought. It will get Caio the help he needs as he waits for a kidney transplant. She thanked God. With Him she still spoke Portuguese: *Obrigado, Deus.*

5

While digging through her purse for a piece of gum, Larissa notices her blinking phone. She has two messages. The first one is from Mrs. Chaffey: "Hi, Larissa. Hope this finds you well. How are you? Just calling to check in. Haven't heard from you in a couple of days, and I know you haven't been feeling all that well. Is there anything I can do? Anything at all? Are you okay with money? I think I told you—yes, I'm sure I did—about the appointment with Dr. Thatcher on Wednesday. Remember we moved the time from

11:30 to 10:30. Do you want to carpool with us? We can pick you up on the way . . ."

Larissa hangs up as an announcement pops from the loudspeakers. Her heart gallops. She taps her right foot on the ground and repeatedly brings her knees together and apart.

6

For four months now, these guttural pains, these notions stayed with her and intensified. As she approached the Chaffeys' home for another check-in, she saw Mr. Chaffey yell at a boy for riding his bike too close to his car. She tucked behind a neighbor's cypress and crouched down. The timbre of his scream was menacing, and what worried her most was how gentle he was once she buzzed the doorbell, fetching her water and an orange—even peeling it for her, in one long coil—with a smile on his face. He'd gotten so skilled, Larissa thought, at camouflaging his rage that even she'd missed it at first. Mrs. Chaffey was *still* oblivious, or maybe just resigned, but now Larissa could spot it, flickering just beyond the rims of his blue irises, like pilot lights, always burning.

7

At twenty-seven, Larissa has known and seen plenty of pregnant women, and they've always been quick to let her know how difficult the process can be, but so far, Larissa has enjoyed the course. Morning sickness hasn't been an issue, and routine moments, like making herself farofa, seem to carry extra importance as she cooks for two. She especially likes when she can feel her baby's movements, which her doctor calls *quickenings.* Her baby always strikes the same spot, an inch left of her belly button, and the whole time, she smiles. It's as if she and the baby speak a tacit language, one in which only the two of them are fluent.

8

Just two days ago, Mrs. Chaffey and Larissa spoke and laughed, discussed cravings and kickings. The phone rang, and Mrs. Chaffey chased it down, her bare feet pounding on the hardwood floor, rattling the dishes in the buffet. "Coming! Coming!" she said, as if her words would somehow carry to the caller. Larissa had sipped her herbal tea and stared out the small kitchen window over the sink. Mr. Chaffey was gardening in his pajama bottoms, no shoes, and bare chested. He leaned against a sharp shovel whose blade reflected a spot of sun.

The symptoms of her foreboding returned: Coolness oozed over Larissa in the usual progression, starting at the small of her back, spiraling outward to the top of her spine till it reached her neck, making her shiver. Her stomach simmered, and she dumped the rest of her tea into the sink.

Minutes passed.

She was wrong.

And glad.

Just as the presentiment lifted and relief began to overtake her limbs, a garter snake that was no wider than a shoelace slithered through the backyard's deep dirt grooves, away from Mr. Chaffey. Without hesitation, he tracked it down, plodding on bits of dry soil. Curls of rich dust floated upward. He closed in on the snake as it neared a thicket of rosemary. Just before the snake could reach safety, he cocked his shovel back and speared the olive-green creature. He managed to cut the snake in almost perfect halves, and both segments quivered for a few seconds before falling still.

Saliva pooled in Larissa's throat. She couldn't swallow.

66

Mr. Chaffey turned her way but didn't bring his eyes to the kitchen window. A gleam shone off his face—an air of pride, as if he wanted people to take notice of his accomplishment.

9

She presses her phone to her ear and listens to the second message. Again, it's Mrs. Chaffey. "Hi, Larissa. It's me. Not sure if you got my other message. Are you okay? I have to admit, I just stopped by your place and used the spare key you gave me. I just wanted to make sure you weren't sick or something. You weren't there, and it was pretty early in the morning. I tidied up a bit, too. Sorry, just couldn't help it. There were lots of towels on the floor and clothes scattered everywhere. I even put a load of laundry in for you. Hopefully, by the time you get home, it'll be done. Anyhow, call me."

Larissa gazes out the large window that showcases a sunlit runway. Jets are stationary one moment, then blasting forward and lifting into the air. Wheels tuck back into the planes' shells instantly after takeoff. Pilots don't give themselves second chances. They know the engines are capable. They know physics is on their side. And if tons of steel and fuel and people can soar across the atmosphere, rip through clouds, and evade the sun, then maybe, Larissa thinks, this is possible, too.

An airline employee who wears a cocked beret that is pinned into her brown locks speaks: "At this time, we'd like to invite our premier fliers, service members, and families with small children to board first."

With her phone in hand, Larissa gets up and leans against her seat. She wiggles her numbing toes and plucks her ticket from her purse, where her fingers also come into contact with a sharp piece of paper. It's her copy of the contract from the Chaffeys, crinkled and creased, the words *gestational surrogate* are bolded as well as *80,000 dollars*. She wraps her phone in the document and drops them both into a trash can, savoring the pop as they strike an aluminum can. She knows it's someone else's sperm, someone else's egg, but she believes—and always will—that biology comes second to humanity.

Brazil is not far now. The smell of pork fat in feijoada and the bright punch of motorbikes' gasoline feel close. She can see Caio's chin dimple and her mother's chipped smile.

"Now boarding passengers in Group B," the woman says. "Group B." Larissa heads to the front of the line, clutching her duffel. She hands her ticket to the attendant, and the woman drags the barcode across the scanner. The beep is sharp and rings in Larissa's ears. "Have a nice flight," the woman says. "And congratulations."

Larissa smiles, stands tall, and begins the long walk through the loading bridge.

PAROLE

After an hour bus ride from the halfway house to West Des Moines, I unload from the back, and shuffle by other passengers who have no idea where I've been and what I've done. There's even this little girl, maybe nine, with bright teeth that reminds me of my little sister around that age. The girl smiles at me as I pass through the aisle carrying nothing but gloves and a little spending cash for the ride back "home" in a few hours. I'm encouraged by the girl's grin, like maybe I got a shot at being free—and not just in the literal sense.

According to my calculations, he lives about a mile into town, which is a lot for me, a seventy-one-year-old man with a weak heart, but it's been decades since I've been able to walk in any direction I choose for more than a minute, so I don't mind. One foot in front of the other. One plodding step at a time.

What's the next step here? Do I try and find myself a little job? Something easy? If there are any spots that are hiring an elderly convict, I'm not so sure I want to work there. I mean if *I'm* a catch—how bad are the other applicants?

I don't want to upset him with this drop-in. Hell, even in my free days, I hated the drop-in. People at the door, ringing the bell, and all of a sudden, you're fetching cake and pulling out chairs and brewing pots of coffee. I always thought of my welcome mat as sarcastic.

No, all I want to do is look at him. I went to prison when I was thirty-one, and my then-girlfriend, Carrie, was pregnant with him. I never got to meet my boy. I never got to hold or smell him. He never visited, and that made sense—a boy should worry about girls and motorcycles, not have to visit his old man in a building meshed of concrete and steel.

I plan to ring his doorbell and ask to see Mr. Larin. (That was the name of my woodshop teacher in high school, and I like the sound of it.) I hope my boy will answer the door, but if he doesn't, maybe his wife will, and while she's explaining that I'm not at the right residence, he'll come up and see what's going on. I'll try to keep the conversation going for a bit, say things like, "Do you know where Mr. Larin lives?" and "Did he *used* to live here?" With all my questions, I could possibly keep them on the stoop for a couple of minutes. They might—*my boy* might—be very friendly, too. He might invite me in to use the phone and get out some pie and Sanka. Do people still drink Sanka? I hope the apple falls far from the tree, though, and when I pass by, he's out with his family on the porch, running a paring knife through a pumpkin's toothy smile, doing whatever it takes to make his kids laugh.

I wrote him letters when I was away. Always a nickname guy, I called him Baby Lou in every one. He never responded, though. In fact, I bet Carrie intercepted my notes, and I don't blame her. I've let it all pass, forgiven everyone with the hope that they would forgive me. Carrie wrote me a few times, mostly to tell me to leave her and Louis alone—that I was a sperm donor, never his pop, and that his new dad was putting in the hard miles: taking him to school, packing his lunch, and teaching him how to change tires. She was right. I was a man far away, in Fort Dodge, who took Bible class twice a week just so God wouldn't shut the door on me. Sometimes, too, on Tuesdays, I'd take a crafts class. There, we built things out of papier-mâché, little sculptures, and all I could think of was how my life was like a wet strip that had never had the time to properly harden.

When I reach Beechtree Drive, the street's not quiet and domestic the way I thought it'd be on a Saturday morning. It's humming with cars and passersby carrying brown boxes and T-shirts and bowls and picture frames. I grab my scrap of paper and check the address. It's the correct house.

A sign that reads ESTATE SALE hangs from the roofline near the front door. The house is big, two stories tall, painted a creamy white with olive-drenched shutters. There are six blue spruce trees in the front yard, all the same distance from each other.

Even though it's chilly out, the front door is wide open, and a man, a worker in a red vest, nods as I pass the threshold. All these people are stomping along the hardwood floors, unsure of what they're searching for, hoping that a mug and a throw rug will make their Saturday better.

The house has a warm smell to it, as if someone has boiled cinnamon sticks. In the foyer, the scent is strong, but it dissipates as I wind toward the living room and stare at a painting over the fireplace of a boat tracing across the sea, its sail full. "A beauty, right?" a woman with a tight face and loose curls says. She also has on a red vest and appears to be working the sale.

"Yes," I say. "Who painted it?"

"It's a Winslow Homer print."

"Nice," I say. "You can almost feel the wind and the ocean's spray, right?"

"I know."

"Where's the owner of the home?" I ask. "Is he moving or something?"

"I think he passed away."

"What?" I say.

The woman taps a coworker who happens to pass by carrying a stack of dishes. "The man who owned this home is dead, right?" she says.

The man nods. "Yeah, a few weeks ago. A heart attack at forty."

I rub my face and feel as though a crack has split around my chest, allowing cold air to seep through and burn the sides of my heart and lungs. This day has kept me going for so long, and I made it, finally, to his home, my shoes aligned on the carpeting where his feet very well could have stood weeks prior. A flare of pain shoots across my rib cage. I clutch my chest, grab hold of the mantel, and count backward from ten.

"Sir? Sir? Are you okay?" the man says.

I gather myself and assure them I'm all right. "And his family?" I say.

"Think he was a lone wolf," the man says. "This whole thing was all set up by his accountant. He did well for himself. I mean this is one nice place, right?"

"Yeah," I say. "It's something." I move about the floor plan. One of the rooms is getting little attention as most of the goodies have been cleared out, so I tuck inside what seems to be my boy's old office. There's wood paneling on the walls, a large bureau in the center, and a closet off to the side stuffed with bowling trophies that signify a perfect game, first prize in a league tournament, and another for third place in a county championship. I never cared much for bowling—any activity you can manage with a cigarette in your mouth hardly seems like a sport—and I know his mother hated it—she often said it ruined her manicures—so I wonder where the love came from, and I wonder how many other loves I missed out on.

A turquoise ball covered with purple swirls rests on the floor, glittering in the soft light that

73

wends through the far window. I brush the ball's smooth surface with my palm.

I was lying earlier when I mentioned the Mr. Larin story. Sure, that was the plan, but if things went to plan, I never would have been incarcerated. I was really hoping that when I rang the bell, Baby Lou would recognize me in some capacity. I wanted something gooey, you know? When you share a cell for forty years, a man finds himself in need of something like that.

I head into the backyard, where a group of people are examining a barbecue. One man lifts the lid, pretends to flip burgers, and laughs while his what-seems-to-be wife howls with laughter, then lets out, "Oh, Leroy! You're a hoot."

I take a seat in an outdoor chair on the deck, and when a worker—the guy who confirmed Lou's passing—comes by and asks me whether I need help, I tell him that I'm testing out the chair. That seems to appease him, and he leaves me alone and files to the far end of the backyard, positioning himself in front of a detached garage, where the door has been lifted and showcases a car that's tucked under a brown cover. He stands near the vehicle, smoking a cigar in perfect rhythm—a puff, an exhale, a flick; a puff, an exhale, a flick. After the man finishes his stogie, he scans the area and tosses the butt far behind the garage.

A short customer approaches the estate sale worker and speaks in a loud voice. "So I'll do what I can to convince my wife and hopefully be back here in a few hours with my good ol' checkbook."

The worker nods, chuckles, extends his hand, and the two men shake on it. "You got it. I'll take the cover off now and store it and the other necessary materials in the trunk," the worker says.

"All right. I like your style," the man says. "Positive thinking." The man turns away, and the worker begins peeling the car cover off the vehicle. As he works, it becomes clear that the car is facing forward, pointing directly out into the long, flat driveway. I can't help but wonder whether the estate sale crew did that, or whether Lou was skilled enough to back his ride up all that way and tuck his expensive car into the tiny garage, but I'm impressed nonetheless.

The worker plucks the cover off the front bumper, giving way to a shimmering silver Porsche convertible with a black cloth top. It's not the car that gets my attention—sure, it's beautiful, in seemingly immaculate condition, and picturing my boy driving around his manicured neighborhood in this drop-top is an image I'll love as long as I can—no, what grabs hold of me and won't let go is the white license plate that dangles from the front bumper, like a loose buck tooth. I am far enough away that I need to squint, but with my eyes narrowed, it's clear: my boy had elected to buy a vanity plate, which allowed seven characters that he'd used to spell out BABYLOU.

I push myself off the rickety chair and shuffle across the grass to the garage, feeling a tingle in my spine and sharp heat in the corners of my eyes. The worker nods as I approach, and I smile back. "A beauty, right? Only thirteen thousand miles, too," he says. "I thought we'd sold it the other day, so I had her resting under the cover, but the buyer just called a little while ago and said he didn't want it, so it's back!"

I crouch to my knees and run my hand over the raised lettering on the front license plate, tracing the voluptuous curves of the *B* and the sharp lines of the *L*. "Baby Lou," I say.

75

"Weird, right?" the worker says. "The new owner—whoever it is—will have to get 'em changed anyway, so it doesn't matter . . ."

"I hear ya."

"Are you in the market?"

"Maybe."

"It's a stunning car. A five-speed, inline six, good amount of horses, and new tires."

"You don't know a thing about cars, do you?" I say.

"Is it that obvious?" the worker says, biting his bottom lip.

"*Good amount of horses* gave you away. Can I take it for a spin?"

"Sure, I just need your driver's license. I'm not allowed to go with you, because my boss won't let us leave the grounds, but you can take it around the block and stuff."

"Oh, I see. Well, I don't have a license."

"Really?"

"Yeah."

"Don't drive anymore?"

"No, I shot a store clerk at a liquor store forty years ago. Never got around to renewing it."

The worker's eyes open wide, and he inspects my lips, cheeks, and nose as though he is going to bring out a pad and sketch me. Then he grabs his fishbowl belly and laughs. "Good one," he says. "Same here!"

"Two peas in a pod," I say.

The worker sucks his teeth, then says, "But, yeah, if you don't have a license, I can't let you take the car."

"Fair enough. Can I at least sit in it?"

"Of course. Your shoes clean?"

I nod, open the driver's-side door, and plop into the leather bucket seat that wraps my thighs and supports my spine in a simultaneously firm-and-soft way. A warm combination of coffee, maybe some cinnamon, stays with me in the cabin, and with each inhale, I suck the bitter scent into my nostrils, savoring the flavor, almost tasting it as it collides with my tongue.

I depress the clutch and slide the shifter from first to second, then from third to fourth, and up into fifth.

The worker bends down to the level of the open passenger-side window. "Looks good on you," he says. "Like you've been here before."

The world is heavy with quiet, as if I'm deep in the ocean, young, free. In this moment, I haven't gotten drunk on March 1st, 1983; I haven't had a fight with Carrie about the rent and how I couldn't pull my weight; I haven't wandered down the road and brought my pistol. I haven't gotten scared and fired a round into the chest of the young clerk behind the counter for a measly forty-six dollars.

At the end of your life, if you've had a total of ten hours of sheer, unbridled joy, then you've done something right. All I want now is to collect some hours so that when the lights go black, I'll know I've kissed a woman, hummed some tunes, and spent some time in whatever way possible with my son.

With the car key glinting on the dashboard, I take hold of my chest and begin to gasp, shake, and flicker my eyes. "Help," I whisper.

The worker peeks back inside, and when I see I have him, I crank up the intensity: I let my eyes roll back and rip open my shirt, causing a button to pop off and tap against the windshield. "Go get my wife," I say.

"She has what I need! Please! Hurry! Her name is Barbara."

The worker says a few jumbled words and darts from the garage, his feet banging on the polished asphalt floor, then the gravel, and then the grass. I sit up, straighten my shirt, grab the key with the rabbit's-foot chain from the dash, and jam it into the ignition.

A roar comes up and surrounds the car, echoing in the tiny one-car garage. The attendees of the estate sale all turn around in unison, their eyes lining up on the silver Porsche that rattles in its cage with plumes of exhaust pushing from its pipes and coiling around its frame.

I tear out of the driveway, let first gear redline around six-thousand, and am swinging into the road by the time I pull the shifter into second. My back's alive with cylindrical reverberations, and I can't hear anything but the push of the engine. Alongside the car, hedges, mailboxes, and picket fences blur into one gorgeous swath. I keep my feet hard on the pedals and my hands tight on the steering wheel, where me and my boy's fingerprints get to live with each other for at least a half a tank.

LOVE AT SIX

Zachary had been in his room all evening.

Mary Ann kept tiptoeing over to his quarters and pressing her ear to the door. She thought she could hear her grandson cry. "Sweetie," she said, taking a step back, "are you okay?" She returned her right ear to the door. Zachary didn't answer. "Can I come in?" she asked. Mary Ann loved her grandson but couldn't stand when things got tricky like this. She only got to see him every other month, when his mother would drive him up from Vermont, so she felt a little out of sorts when the seas got rough. It was especially hard to do without Tobias around. He was always better at solving problems. "Zachary? Can I come in? Do you want dinner? Do you want me to read you a bedtime story?" There was no answer. "Did you have a good time today? I thought we had such a good time."

Finally, she turned the handle and opened the door to her guest room. Zachary had been scared to sleep on such a high bed, so she'd piled a bunch of blankets on the floor in front of the fireplace. He was twisted on his side, crying. Next to him was a stuffed animal, an old Rottweiler that was missing his nose. She'd only seen Zachary cry once before, when he'd fallen from a tree in her daughter's backyard, but these tears, she thought, had nothing to do with physical discomfort.

In time, she managed to lower herself to the ground and curl up next to Zachary. He didn't budge, but she was thrilled that he took her hand and rubbed it. The meeting of two such things—young and old skin—made her happy. "Did you have a good day today?" she asked. "Are you okay?"

"Kind of," Zachary said. He turned his head and lined his gaze with Mary Ann's. His eyes were glassy, and tears had left the tops of his cheeks shiny.

"What do you mean 'kind of'? Ever since you got off the phone with your mom, you've been quiet. Then you came in here and didn't even have supper. The grilled cheese I made you is cold, and the tomato bisque looks ugly."

"I'm sorry," he said, flopping onto his back and shutting his eyes. His lids pushed out the remaining tears, and he erased them with his knuckles.

"It's all right. I can make you another one if you feel like it. The first one wasn't that good, anyway. Maybe I can do better." She'd gotten along without Tobias these past two years and was proud of that, but sometimes having a person in the house made it hard, as she found herself taking care of someone and recalled bringing Tobias soup in bed and scanning his back for bedsores. She missed him so much that it was best she didn't think of him and how happy he'd made her. It'd been years since someone had kissed her goodnight and whispered, "I love you," and it seemed as if the words were on the verge of extinction.

"What happened on the phone with your mother? Did you tell her how much fun we had at the lighthouse? How we may have seen a shark? I think it was a shark. Don't you? Wasn't it great? Up so high? And we were so lucky that the nice man was there and that he opened up the stairs and led us to the top. You know, I've been there maybe twenty times, but never to the top. You have to be someone special to go up there. Maybe they saw you, and that's why they allowed it."

Zachary laughed. Mary Ann continued to stroke his fingers.

"It was a perfect day," he said. "I love the lighthouse. I really do. It's so tall, and I love that it's painted like a candy cane. Why do they make them like that? Is it so ships can see them from far away?"

"I don't know. They're not always striped. We should have asked the park ranger. He would've known. Are you warm enough? Do you have enough blankets? Are you homesick? Do you want to go home? You know tomorrow it's supposed to be another beautiful day, and we can go to the botanical gardens and feed the ducks. I've got some stale bread that they'll really like."

"Why don't we buy them good bread?"

"I hear they like stale bread better."

"Really?"

Mary Ann nodded. She moved her hand to his belly and patted his soft flesh. She didn't *see* her daughter in Zachary, but she could *hear* her—the curiosity and innocence. "Do you want me to put on a fire for you, like last night?"

"Yes, please."

"It wasn't too hot?"

"It was hot, but I liked the sound, and I didn't need a nightlight because the flames were so big."

Rarely did she make a fire these days, even when the Maine winters were harsh. Tobias had installed the best heating system, so she just pressed the lever to the right when the temperature dropped, but she knew that all heat wasn't created equal and that a fire was still king, especially in the eyes of a child.

Zachary and his mother lived in an apartment in Montpelier, and it didn't have a fireplace. Last night, when Mary Ann had gotten up to fetch a glass of water, she'd peeked into the guest bedroom and spotted Zachary, sitting up, a few feet from the fire.

The image had warmed her as much as the flickers themselves.

As she piled the wood in a heap, she turned back and glanced at Zachary. He was smiling now, and his eyes were bright and clear. "So," Mary Ann said, "what happened on the phone with your mother?"

"I told her that I want to work in a lighthouse when I grow up," he said.

"Oh, sweetie, that's wonderful." She piled on more wood and pulled a few sheets of newspaper from the adjacent basket. The funnies were dusty and over four years old. She jammed them underneath the grate, struck a match, and then had Zachary bring the fire to the cartoons. "You're so aware and bright—you'll make sure nothing happens to those ships."

"She said it can't happen. That all lighthouses are now automatic or something."

"Is that true?"

"I guess."

"And that's what made you sad?" Mary Ann returned to Zachary, and they both sat, staring at the fire, studying the flames as they bent and twisted through the wood.

"Yes. I was so excited. I knew what I wanted to do with my life and where I wanted to live and how it was all gonna be, and then my stupid mom ruined it all."

"Honey. Honey. It's okay. Shh." Mary Ann scratched his back.

"It all sounded great. I was gonna live in Maine and have a dog, a big dog, maybe a St. Bernard with one of those little barrels around his neck." He cried some more. His tears came with little buildup. They went from zero to sobbing in moments. "And then. And then . . ." he said.

Mary Ann draped a quilt over Zachary's shoulders. "And then?" she asked. "And then, what?"

"And then my mom told me about you."

Mary Ann's hands quivered, and she pressed her tongue against the roof of her mouth. "Oh, dear," she said. "What about me? Did I do something wrong?" The flames hissed as they reached dry spots in the wood. "If I did, Zachary, I'm deeply sorry. I really am." She worried that their visits would be spaced out even farther now, and that instead of meeting every other month, they would be changed to every three or four months, and that in time, Zachary wouldn't want to make the trek up the Interstate and spend the weekend with her.

He spoke in a weak voice.

"What was that?" Mary Ann asked.

"And then," he said, shaking the quilt from his back, "I told her about you. I told her that I wanted to live in the lighthouse and be with my dog—the St. Bernard—and that I wanted to marry you. I told her that I loved you, and that I wanted you to be my wife, and she told me that I couldn't marry you. That you only marry people you love. And then I told her that I loved you more than any other girl, and she told me that that is a different kind of love. Is it true?"

Mary Ann tried to answer but couldn't. She gazed at Zachary and brushed some of the straight hair from his face and tucked it behind his ears. She swiped her fingers below his eyes and rubbed out the remaining droplets. Smoke built up in the chimney, and the fire began to catch, popping and crackling. "It's true," she said, "but it's a better kind of love, one that's sure to last forever."

Zachary nodded, brought his body closer to Mary Ann's, then dropped his face against her left arm.

84

She kissed the top of his head, drew in his warm scent, and continued to watch the blaze wrap the dry pine.

SHH

Carissa will arrive early and sit in her car in the underground parking garage. She will listen to classic rock and wait for her husband, Jim. Who sings this song? she'll wonder. The Carpenters? Bread? America? She will inspect herself in the rearview mirror and notice that her cheeks have blanched.

She'll unfasten her seatbelt and study a daddy longlegs tiptoeing across the dashboard. With a quick slap, she'll crush the spider, flick its body to the car floor, and pull her hand back. Some guts and a single leg with a delicate bend will stick to her palm, and she'll wipe them hard across her jeans.

***

A few months ago, Carissa and Jim lay in bed: Jim on top of the sheets, flipping through another medical brochure, and Carissa tucked in on her side, facing the wall, studying the faded roses on the wallpaper.

"Maybe I could have more tests done," Jim said.

"It's more money, though. We don't have that kind of money. Are you sure you don't want to adopt?" Carissa rolled over and faced Jim.

"That's really expensive, too," he said. "Plus, I could never love someone else's child the way I'd love my own."

"But the doctor said there's, like, a one percent chance. Less, actually." She felt her cheeks warm. They'd been having this conversation for over a year now. She didn't know what else to say.

Jim let out a big breath, causing a loose feather from the comforter to take flight. Carissa studied the

87

grayish plume as it swayed back and forth and eventually settled near the foot of her dresser. She'd always thought that Jim wasn't a typical man—that was what she loved most about him. He was vulnerable; he spoke the truth, admitted his shortcomings, cried at romantic films, and penned tender notes to her for little reason, but his reaction to his weak seminal vesicles was too trite for her to believe: It was as though not being able to make a human had made him less of one. Just the other day while slathering his face with Brut, he'd said, "Look at me. I do it all. I shave. I work construction. I do everything manly. But that's the problem. I only *look* like a man." She'd tried to console him, but he'd pulled away.

"Night," Carissa said. She closed her eyes, and minutes later, Jim clicked off the light.

Their relationship had always been an unbroken boulevard of green lights, and this was the first *real* problem they'd had in thirteen years—seven of dating and six of marriage—and Carissa wondered how and whether it would ever be resolved.

With her head nuzzled against the pillow and the ebb and flow of Jim's breath filling the room, she thought about those nights when they'd open a bottle of cheap wine and talk about their baby. Blair for a boy; Grace for a girl. They'd talk about where they'd move to get away from the drippy faucets and noisy neighbors of the one-bedroom on Western Avenue. "A small place, maybe by the beach, the sand between our toes," Jim would say. They'd smile and make love because they wanted to. As an expression of love and desire.

She turned toward Jim. They hadn't closed the blinds tightly, so a bit of streetlamp light spilled onto Jim's face. His eyes were shut, and his nostrils flared as he pushed out breath after breath. His hands were atop the covers, and Carissa intertwined her fingers with his and felt flecks of paint on his nails from the recent construction job. She snuggled up closer to him, erasing the empty space between them.

***

The next morning, a phone call came in early, waking them both. Carissa hopped out of bed and snatched the phone from the receiver. The businesslike woman on the other end of the line explained that a third grade teacher at Franklin Elementary was sick and that the school needed Carissa to sub. Carissa tried to sound as though she'd been up for hours. She agreed and hung up the phone.

"Which school?" Jim asked, sitting up in bed.

"Franklin."

"Oh, good. You love that one," he said. The skin around his eyes was dark, almost purple. "What grade?"

"Third." Carissa plucked a navy suit from her closet and paired it with a billowy blouse.

"You know, last night I was reading about things I can eat and drink that can make my sperm stronger," Jim said. "Couldn't hurt to try. A lot of Eastern-medicine stuff."

"Yeah?" Carissa said. She scurried over to Jim and grabbed hold of her hair so that he could fasten the latch on her necklace.

"You look great, beautiful."

Carissa spun around and let her hair go. Locks fell to her back and alongside her shoulders. "When are you heading off?" she asked.

"Around eight. Not allowed to start construction in this one town until about that time.

The neighbors call the police every time we try to get a jump on things. I'll head over to the health food store after and ask them about these herbs and stuff. You want to see the brochure?"

"Not now," Carissa said. She headed to the bathroom, gargled some mouthwash, and spritzed perfume from a sample-sized bottle.

"Those kids are lucky to have you. So lucky. I love you."

Carissa reached out and squeezed Jim's hands. "Me too." She flung her purse over her shoulder and searched for her keys.

***

Carissa hurried into the office at Franklin Elementary. Trophies from spelling bees and soccer tournaments glittered in wooden cases by the entrance. Teachers checked their mailboxes, sipped coffee, and gibbered with one another. Carissa stood, waiting patiently behind a woman and a little boy for the secretary, Ms. Watters. The woman held the hand of the boy, whose hair was straight and whose feet were strapped into Velcro shoes. The woman then thanked Ms. Watters and headed down the hall. "You're gonna be fine," the woman said. "Remember Mommy will come pick you up at two, and we'll go get a smoothie." Carissa studied the boy and the woman as they walked down the corridor and grew smaller and smaller.

"Hi, Ms. Watters," Carissa said. Ms. Watters had a round face with a ruddy complexion. Even a few feet away, Carissa could detect the chemical smell of hairspray. "I'm Mrs. Vega."

"Oh, yes. Good morning, Mrs. Vega. Wow, you made it here fast."

"I drove like an animal." She didn't know why she'd said that. She thought of an animal behind the wheel of her red Pontiac, a cavalier raccoon who didn't care to wear his seatbelt, and she tightened her mouth to keep from laughing.

Ms. Watters asked Carissa to follow her and showed her to the classroom. "You're a lifesaver," Ms. Watters said. "The other third grade teachers will be coming by to show you where they are in the books and what they're doing. The bell will ring in about ten minutes. Thanks again!"

Carissa walked inside the classroom and shut the door behind her. The lights were already on, and a rose-scented deodorizer emitted an artificial garden smell. She paced the classroom. Desks were arranged in five groups of four. Dreamcatchers hung from the ceiling. Posters plastered the back wall: one of a boy picking up a person's wallet with the tagline "Character is what you do when no one is looking," and another of Garfield holding a pencil in his chubby mitt, with "Do the *Write* Thing" in perfect cursive underneath him.

She penned her name on the whiteboard. It felt right to stand in front of the classroom once again. She read the attendance log and scanned the students' names. Then she pictured the children seated at their desks, hands folded, all gazing her way.

***

Jim will text her. "Running late. Be there soon. Love you." Carissa will turn the volume up on her car stereo and take a few seconds before texting him back. She will lower her car seat till she is practically horizontal, clench her jaw, and dig her fingers into her palm to keep her hands from shaking.

91

The real classroom teacher had been diagnosed with the flu and would be out for at least a week, so Carissa subbed again. It was lunchtime, and she snacked on some baked chips and water. She thought about Jim. He was less harried last night. He hadn't read any brochures, but he had brought home ground coriander seeds, the juice of yohimbe bark, and a boomerang-shaped piece of something called maca root.

From outside, the giggles and screams of students on the playground wafted through the walls along with the thump of jump ropes and basketballs against the blacktop.

The door opened. "Carissa?" a voice said.

"Hi," Carissa said, turning toward the door, surprised to have a visitor.

"I'm Ethan." He wore a black sweater from which a white dress shirt poked free at the collar and cuffs. His skin was dewy, and he had sizable dimples under his light beard. His smile was bright, and it looked as though he'd slept well. Carissa got up from her chair, and the two of them shook hands. A firm shake, she thought. "So sorry I didn't make it over here yesterday. I thought another teacher was going to help you out. Anyhow," he said, fetching her teachers' edition from the back counter. "Here's where we are. It's a story called *A Cloak for the Dreamer*. A very good one."

"Okay, yes," she said. "The students have been helping me find my way. They're very sweet."

Ethan explained what the students were having trouble with and places where she could really dive into the text. He also told her that if she had any problems, she could send a troublemaker his way.

There was something confident about Ethan. Assured, not cocky. She combed over his pink lips and took in the whites of his eyes. "Are you the third grade chair?" she asked.

"Yes."

"Wow. And so young."

Ethan dropped his gaze toward the floor and laughed. "Twenty-six. Is that *so* young? A hundred years ago, I would've already had a wife, three kids, and tuberculosis." He placed his tongue between his teeth. "I know it's polite to return a question with a question, but in this case, I won't."

"I'm thirty-one."

"You look younger than I do."

"You're sweet. And maybe need glasses."

"Anything else I can help you with? I mean, I'll be around, but anything you want to ask me about the lesson plans, math, science, P.E.?"

"No, everything's fine."

"All right. See you around." Ethan smiled and walked out the door.

Carissa took a breath. She inspected herself in a window's reflection. Her hydrated skin beamed, and she liked the way a wisp of hair cascaded perfectly onto her brow.

When the bell rang, the students lined up outside the classroom. A rush of energy flooded her body, and she was glad to know she could still feel this way. At home, she was antsy, surrounded by brochures rife with scary sentences; here, at school, she stood up front, with twenty sets of eyes on her, holding the answer key.

***

She ambled to her apartment building. Thoughts bounced around her mind: students, lesson plans, discipline, and Ethan. His poise was something she hadn't seen since her father. Her dad was a Delta pilot, and he always came home from his usual flight—LA to DC—wearing a stiff blue uniform and an easy smile.

Jim stood in the kitchen, scrubbing his hands. On the counter were more baggies of powders and capsules. "So, day two," he said. "How'd it go?"

"You bought more of this stuff?" Carissa removed her earrings.

"Yeah, this is saw palmetto. It's supposed to work wonders. The guy said it can really enhance the strength of sperm."

She came up behind him and rubbed his shoulders. Out the kitchen window, cranes hauled crates into the air, and smoke rose from stacks at the Long Beach port. "Seems good," she said.

Jim dumped out the contents of one bag onto the counter. Capsules rolled around, nestling in the dirty grout between tiles. He told Carissa about each herb, and she enjoyed seeing him come to life a little. He really thought this would work. Everything had happened at the same time for Jim: his mother had passed, his hours were cut, and he'd found out that his sperm had both low motility and potency. Sometimes Carissa wondered, What if I told him I was pregnant? How would he react? Would he pick me up and swing me over his shoulder like he used to?

They talked a bit about school and about the roof that Jim was repairing. "I was working with this man from Guadalajara, and he had all these roses tattooed on his arms. We didn't have much to talk about, so I asked him about the tattoos, and he told me that each flower was for one of his children. Eight roses. Eight."

The conversation always ended up at children. Carissa nodded and placed a skillet over the burner, got the cast iron real hot, and then dropped in two chicken breasts. Steam curled to the ceiling as she watched the day morph to dusk. She leaned against the counter. Her hairdresser had once told her that men married women hoping they'd never change, and that women married men hoping they would.

Jim shuffled into the other room and watched TV with the volume high. Piped-in laughter from a sitcom mixed with the sizzle in the kitchen. She wondered where Ethan lived. Where he grew up. What his parents were like. Did he have a wife? Children?

***

Carissa will wait for Jim for ten more minutes. Then she will get out of her car and walk up the stairs, clutching the banister. She'll take to the long corridor and scan the doors' golden signs, searching for Dr. Michalski.

***

The meal was quiet with just the sounds of forks and knives against cheap plates and the consistent buzzing from the electrical poles outside. This was Carissa's biggest fear: that she and Jim would get used to this phase of their lives and that difficult times would become normal.

"Really delicious, hun," Jim said, gathering some grains of rice on his fork. Carissa watched his gaze leave her face and brush over the heaps of herbs on the counter. He started to speak, but his voice was soft. He tried again. "Do you think this will work? All this stuff."

The query hung in the air while Carissa searched for the right answer. She pretended she was chewing and held up her forefinger. "Stranger things have happened," she said, unable to believe that that was the best response she could come up with. "I just . . ." She wanted to say, I just want you to be the way you were not that long ago, when you didn't feel sorry for yourself, when *I* was the one who could break down and seek comfort.

"You just . . ."

"I just want you to be happy. Can you be happy?"

"Happy?"

"Yes. You can't make this define you."

Jim angled his head toward the placemat and shooed away some crumbs. The two of them sat there a while longer, silent.

***

The next morning, Carissa arrived at school early. She planned the day's lesson and picked at a moth hole on her right sleeve. She graded spelling tests from the day before. Practically every student had scored a nine out of ten, and she thought she'd start the day by having them each correctly write the word *beginning* in their notebooks.

"Good morning," a voice said. She hadn't heard the door open, but when she looked over, Ethan was standing near the front of the classroom, clutching a blue "World's Greatest Grandma" mug. He was clean shaven today, giving him a boyish air. "How are things?" He approached the kidney-shaped table and sat across from Carissa.

96

"Going well. Just doing some grading."

He took a sip. "How long have you been teaching?"

Carissa squinted and tried to decipher the design on Ethan's tie. Wolves, she thought, little wolves with their heads tipped back, howling. "Just started, really. Career change." She shrugged.

"That's why you're so good."

"Oh, I don't know about that."

"I do. You're the only sub we've had that knows what the hell is going on."

"I do what I can," she said.

"And you do it well."

The air conditioning kicked on, and a gust blasted hard enough to set a few dust bunnies free from the overhead lights. Carissa watched one of them flit about the room behind Ethan while he continued to drink from his mug.

They discussed routine topics: living in Los Angeles, their dislike for the catty teachers' lounge, and the love they had for their students. She wondered why Ethan was here, and she wondered when he'd get down to business and tell her what was scheduled for today. After some time, she realized that he wasn't there to do anything but chat.

"Are you married?" he asked.

"Yes. You?"

"Still looking." He smiled. The coffee had left his teeth an amber color. "Still looking . . ."

"What about the three kids and tuberculosis?"

"Ah, yes, the dream."

"So, what's this ideal woman look like?"

"Hmm."

"You have to know before you can get it."

"Well," he said, "I guess—"

There was a knock on the classroom door.

Carissa pushed out her chair and glanced at the clock. She still had a little time before the bell was to ring. She yanked the door open. One of her students, a little boy named Patricio, stood still. His nose was bleeding, and his head was tilted back.

"Oh, God," Carissa said. "Come in."

"The nurse isn't there?" Ethan said.

"It's okay," Carissa said.

Ethan popped up and fetched a large box of tissues. He pulled out his chair and guided the student into his seat. Carissa squeezed her water bottle, causing a stream to burst onto some paper towels; then she cleaned a rivulet of dried blood atop Patricio's lips. The boy's nose continued to ooze, and he shut his eyes while Ethan and Carissa worked on him. Since the bleeding wouldn't stop, they decided to roll tissues like cigars and slide them into the boy's nostrils. "We may have to amputate," Ethan said a few times, causing Patricio to laugh. When the boy's nose finally clotted, he jumped up and wobbled toward the door. Because of the tissues in his nostrils, he muttered a strange-sounding, "Thanks." Ethan and Carissa laughed, shook their heads, and headed over to the sink, where they scrubbed their hands, let the hot water coat their skin, and worked soap into lather. Traces of blood swirled, joined the suds, and turned from red to pink as they mixed with the water and headed down the drain.

***

Just as Carissa finds Dr. Michalski's office and is about to turn the brass knob, she will hear her phone chime. It will be another text from Jim. "Here! Finally!" the text will read. She will head back down the hall and wait for him in front of the elevator.

***

The teacher Carissa was replacing was still ill when Friday came around, and Carissa found herself rooting for the flu, hoping that she'd be able to keep this job for a while longer. It did her good to be out of the house, distracted with a job, and it also gave her time to prove to the faculty and administration of Franklin Elementary that she was worthy of a teaching position, should something open up. She found herself being a bit fawning, too, laughing at the principal's puns during the opening announcements and complimenting the secretary's sweater, knowing full well that she would never buy a cardigan, even at a heavy discount.

She ran off multiplication worksheets in the teachers' lounge. The photocopier's racket was oddly comforting, and she thought more about the conversation she'd had with Jim. He was becoming increasingly despondent, and he smelled bad. Usually, he was quick to take to the bathroom, wrap himself with soapy bubbles, and emerge minutes later smelling oaky, with ribbons of steam spiraling from his shoulders. When she'd let him know of his odor, he'd snapped, telling her he had no reason to look or smell nice. "It's a roof," he'd shouted. "I'm working on a fucking roof!" She hadn't cried in front of him, staying stoic until she reached her car.

"Hey!" she heard a voice call out.

"Jesus!" Carissa said. "You scared me. I was in my own little world."

Ethan held two mugs of coffee close to his chest. "Went by your classroom and couldn't find you. Thought you might be in here. This is something I thought I'd never see: a sub running stuff off." He passed her a cup. "Just brewed it."

99

"Thank you," Carissa said. She took the mug by the cup itself, and the heat spread into her palm.

"You all right? You look a—"

"Yes. I'm fine."

"Happy hour tonight. You coming?" Ethan peered down at the front of his dress shirt and noticed that his buttons weren't fastened correctly, so he undid a few and then refastened them.

"No, I don't think so."

"It's at the Catalina Cantina. You know it?"

"Yes," she said. She picked up her papers from the tray, nodded, and left the teachers' lounge with Ethan. The multiplication worksheets stayed warm all the way to her classroom.

"You make coming to work better," Ethan said. "I wasn't so pissed when the alarm clock buzzed."

Her lips rounded into a smile, and her cheeks flushed.

***

Carissa was pleased that the last class of the day on Friday was P.E. because the students were fidgety and needed to run. As soon as the clock read two thirty, she led them to the field and let them play kickball. She assigned each student a number and divided them into two teams—odds and evens—proud that she'd managed to combine a little of the day's math lesson with physical activity. Then, she leaned against the backstop and let the game unfold. Patricio was up, and the whole class *oohed* and *aahed*. Apparently, he had quite the reputation. When the ball was rolled to home plate, he let it go, taking the strike, waiting for the perfect pitch. "No bouncies," he called out. "Too much bounce." Finally, on the third pitch, he saw something he liked and crushed the rubber ball with his right

100

Nike. He stood back, hands on his hips, and wallowed in his feat. The red ball arched high over the field and, at its apex, lined up with the sun, like an eclipse. Carissa couldn't understand why, but the moment filled her with deep pleasure. She was warm in the sun, happy, free, and she enjoyed gazing at Patricio as he rounded the bases, dirt popping free with his solid strides, his arms high above his head.

When she checked the time on her phone, she noticed that Jim had sent her a text: he wouldn't be home for hours because of a roofing problem. She assumed cell phone use wasn't permitted on campus, so she craned her neck and made sure no one important was around, then typed fast: "No problem. Love you." She slid her phone back into her pocket and waited for the bell to ring.

***

The elevator will reach level three, ding, and its doors will part. "Carissa!" Jim will say. "So sorry I'm late. Are you nervous? I've been full of butterflies all day. You too? Are you full of butterflies?" Carissa will smile, and Jim will reach for her hand. "Dr. Michalski's office is this way," she'll say.

***

She parked a little ways from the Catalina Cantina in an oil-splattered spot and made her way to the front door. She yanked on the maraca-shaped handle and headed inside. A flood of mariachi music worked its way to her ears as she strolled the polished tile. Ethan and a few other teachers spoke in loud voices at a nearby table. "Hey!" he called out when he noticed her.

101

"You made it!" He took a slug of his margarita and then wiped some coarse grains of salt from his lips.

"Hi," some of the other teachers said to her, while others offered polite waves and smiles. The vice principal, Mr. Millington, was there, and just as Carissa began to lift her hand up, spread her fingers, and swing her wrist, the vice principal crunched down on a tortilla chip and some salsa squirted onto his tie. Carissa took a seat at the head of the table. Ethan was to her left, and to her right was a chair piled with jackets and purses. Directly on the wall in front of her was a Diego Rivera painting of a little girl hugging— or maybe gathering—hundreds of lilies. Carissa inspected the curves of the petals and bright yellows of the stamens. Was the girl's nose capable of pulling in all that scent?

In time, Ethan cut himself off from the group's conversation—they were discussing what Franklin looked like before the remodel—and turned to Carissa. He seemed more casual, with his shirtsleeves rolled up showcasing his hairy arms and tanned skin. "I feel weird here," Carissa said. "I'm not one of you guys. I mean, why would a sub come to happy hour?"

"Because I invited you," Ethan said. He scooted his chair closer to Carissa, till his pant leg brushed against her knee. The fabric was light and smooth, and after a few seconds, she could no longer feel him. The waiter came by as one of the teachers delivered a joke. After the laughter softened, she leaned toward the server and ordered a margarita on the rocks without salt. Ethan ordered another, too. "I have an idea," he whispered.

"What?"

"After this, we should go to Mrs. Alvarez's house. She's the real third grade teacher, and I know where she lives. We can tell her that she'd better be sick next week. What do you think? We can take her around and make her lick doorknobs and payphones."

Carissa laughed. "Do they even have payphones anymore?"

"Sure they do." Ethan's breath was strong with booze and salsa. They simultaneously reached for a chip, and their fingers met in the salty bowl.

"I'm sad to be going next week, too. I've really enjoyed working at Franklin. Working with you. Do you think they'll have any openings in the fall? Do you know of anyone retiring or leaving town?"

"No, not really. I'm sure you're at the top of the list. Hell, I think even the kids want you to stay, and not because you're the usual pushover sub, but 'cause they really like you. And they really hate Mrs. Alvarez. Everyone really likes you. *I* really like you."

She let the compliment wash over her. Was she as red as she thought she was? She brought the heel of her hand to her forehead to test whether her skin was clammy. Carissa had gotten used to pain at the top of her spine, a sharp twinge that had settled between her shoulder blades. Doctors and chiropractors had assured her it wasn't serious—just a result of poor posture and stress. But as she took another sip of alcohol and arched her back, she noticed that the ache had disappeared. Again and again, she rounded her shoulders, twisted in her seat, and couldn't discern the faintest twinge. Ethan asked the waiter for another bowl of chips and clinked Carissa's glass for the third time. Was she more desirable than she thought? Would she be attracted to Jim if she'd met him today? She realized that she hadn't spoken in some time. "I really like being at Franklin," she finally said. "Some really great kids there."

"There are great kids everywhere. Don't you just love it when these little bits of wisdom burst from their mouths? It's like, by not trying to be deep, by just trying to say things in the most honest way possible, they end up being incredibly soulful, you know?"

"You're right," Carissa said. The waiter brought them their margaritas and another bowl of chips. Her gaze hadn't left Ethan's in a few seconds, and when she turned to thank the waiter, her eyes caught a few other members of the table. She was embarrassed to have been so shut off. The vice principal was right there, and she could've been spending time with him, trying to sway him and make him understand that she'd be a perfect fit at Franklin. But she decided against it, telling herself that real work was undercut by brown-nosing. As another teacher spoke, she nodded her head, offered a polite laugh, and returned her eyes to Ethan. She took a sip. "Wow, this one's strong." She coughed a little and took a gulp of water. "Today, this one girl said to me, 'Why do adults always say they're doing well when you ask them how they are? I mean, it's impossible to *always* be well.'"

"She gets it," Ethan said.

"She sees that we're lying."

Ethan laughed. His soft cheeks rose and pushed up into his eyes. "What if adults stopped the bullshit? What if we just said exactly what we felt from here on out? Do you think life would get better?"

"Not at first."

"But eventually, right?"

"I don't know. Caring how others feel is a sign of intelligence and understanding. It's hard to think of just going up to people and saying the truth. There's nothing scarier than honesty."

Beads of sweat had assembled on Ethan's forehead. One in particular slithered between his brows, strangely reminding Carissa of the sperm cells

104

in the brochures that Jim was always studying. Again, she picked up her margarita and took a large pull. The potency of the tequila paired well with the saltiness of the chips.

***

Jim will open the door for Carissa, and she will sign in. There will not be anyone else in the waiting room, nor will there be any attitude from the receptionist for being late. In fact, the woman behind the desk will offer a warm smile. "Dr. Michalski will be right with you," she'll say. Carissa and Jim will sit in two chairs bookended by plastic ferns. Jim will rub Carissa's left knee the way she likes—up and down, up and down— while she flips through an old issue of *Family Circle.*

***

After the second pitcher of margaritas was killed, the other teachers and the vice principal left the table, leaving only Carissa and Ethan. They all handed Ethan the necessary cash—it seemed as if this was the normal protocol—and headed for the door. She heard many of the women say that they had to get back to their families, but Carissa didn't budge. Instead, she sat there calmly and thanked them all for being so gracious and helpful during her time at Franklin.

She knew she, too, should get up, drape her purse over her shoulder, and head out to her car. But she was comfortable. All that waited for her at home was more of the same: Jim, tired, upset—a situation as predictable as sides of the bed. She knew that she'd need to bolster his spirits, and by doing so, lower hers.

"Well, happy weekend," Ethan said.

"How much do I owe?" she asked, trying to find her wallet.

"Let me get this."

"No, please."

"Seriously, I want to. It's been great spending time with you."

"Well, thank you."

Ethan piled all the necessary money in the little leather folder and placed an empty glass atop it. They pushed out their chairs and took to the door with plodding, alcohol-laced footsteps. Jim was probably home by now, eating a peanut butter and jelly sandwich, crumbs falling onto his white shirt while a baseball game played on TV.

Carissa and Ethan were parked near one another, so they headed in the same direction. Ethan walked Carissa to her car and pulled the door open for her. "So," he said, "what are you up to now? Heading home?"

"I guess. Yeah."

"You don't seem too enthralled."

She let out a small puff of air. "No, I'm . . . I'm fine."

"Yeah, when I'm fine, I like to sigh a lot and look depressed, too."

She laughed. "No, I'm just sad it's all over."

"It doesn't have to be."

There was a long silence. A jeep rumbled by with rap music blasting from its open windows and stirred strewn pieces of trash that had collected in the parking lot. A plastic bag lifted off the ground, filled with air, and sailed over a dumpster.

"I think it does. I better be—"

"It's still Friday," Ethan said. "It's still early-ish."

Carissa stared at the ground and grated her shoe against the pavement as if she were stomping out a cigarette. "That's true."

"To sound like one of our students—and get rid of the bullshit filter—do you want to come over and have another drink? Or take an aspirin or something?" He laughed.

Carissa's throat tightened, and she found it hard to swallow. She did want the fun to continue, though. She could have another drink with a colleague, learn some more about the school, the district, and Ethan. "Okay," she said. "Can I follow you?"

Ethan's eyes widened. She thought he looked surprised, most likely believing all those seconds between his question and her answer to be a clear indicator of disinterest. "Um, okay. Yes. Follow the white truck." He cracked his knuckles and rushed to his car. Carissa lowered herself into her Pontiac. She shut the door and buckled her seatbelt.

***

The sky's color faded as Carissa trailed Ethan's truck through crowded streets. Her open window allowed a rush of air to stream over her forehead and cheeks, but it did little to quell her thoughts.

Her cell phone rang. It was Jim's designated ringtone: Thin Lizzy's "The Boys Are Back in Town." The guitar chords resonated strongly in the quiet car. She placed the cell on her lap, answered, and turned on the speakerphone mode. "Hi," she said.

"Hey, where are you? I got home a little while ago."

She had rehearsed what she'd say a few times, so the words came out easily: "Mr. Millington, the vice principal, invited some teachers and me—can you

107

believe it?—to his place for his birthday. A kind of spur-of-the-moment thing. Weird, right?"

"You think he likes you?"

"What?"

"The vice principal. You think he likes you? You think he's gonna hire you?"

"I don't think it can hurt to spend a little more time with him, you know?"

"For sure. Sounds like a great opportunity."

"Yeah, a nice coincidence that I was here for his birthday," she said.

"I don't know if there are such things—maybe everything is already planned out for us." There was a long pause. "I'm pretty beat, and my back's sore as hell. Lots of work today. I'm just gonna kick back here, watch a little TV. There's a pretty decent basketball game on right now, Baylor at . . ." Carissa's thoughts trailed off. Ethan was up ahead, his left blinker pulsing against the night. She concentrated on the turn and swooped hard with him as the light changed to yellow. "Hun? Carissa?"

"Yeah, yeah. I'm here."

"Maybe we can try tonight? If you're up for it? I've been taking the stuff for a few days—who knows?"

She hated that word. *Try.* The act had many synonyms—some beautiful, others ugly—but she never thought it would be reduced to *trying*, as if it were difficult and required effort and focus. "Okay," she said.

"I love you. I really do."

"Me too," she said, hanging up.

＊＊＊

"All right," the secretary will say, "Dr. Michalski will see you now. How are you feeling? Are you nervous?

108

Excited? Swimming in all of it? You're both so cute, you know? Just so sweet looking. There's an innocence about you both. Maybe it's just me being weird. I just see so many couples, and you guys are really something else. Oh, who knows? Maybe I've just had too much coffee or sugar. Right this way. Follow me."

***

The drive to Ethan's felt long, as Carissa passed places that were catalysts for reflection: the pizza place where Jim still had the second-highest score on Ms. Pac-Man; Admiral's Fish House, where she'd gotten sick on sushi and Jim had stayed up with her all night; and Images Movie House, where they'd seen *Godfather I*, *II*, and *III* on a random Wednesday in November.

Ethan made a right, then a left, and they ended up on the Esplanade, only a stone's throw from the Pacific. The ocean played its song, and Carissa listened. Tall apartment buildings faced the sea. Most of the apartments' windows were black, but a few glowed yellow, and she wondered what was going on inside.

Ethan hit the brakes and tucked into the parking garage, while Carissa found a spot out front and pulled curbside. She shut off the engine and listened to the palm fronds stir overhead, their thick, dry blades dancing however the wind instructed. Her hands were moist, and she rubbed them against her skirt, even positioned them in front of the air conditioning vents, hoping that the rush would freeze her sweat. Her eyes burned. Her fingers trembled. If she did nine out of ten things correctly, then she was ninety percent good. Ninety percent. An A. An A minus.

There was a tap on the window. She gasped, brought her hands to her chest, and swallowed.

"So sorry," Ethan said. His words warbled through the glass.

Carissa smiled. Seeing Ethan calmed her—his big, clear eyes, soft complexion, and wavy black hair that was being tousled by the wind. He grinned back, and large dimples appeared on his cheeks. She yanked the handle; he extended a hand, and they headed down the sidewalk to a large building called the Driftwood.

Carissa entered the stairwell. There was pressure in her chest, and her legs felt heavy. As Ethan let go of the door and joined her, she turned back and peeked outside. Her little red Pontiac glimmered in the yellow light of the streetlamps. Even as the metal door began to shut and obstruct her view, she strained to keep her eyes on her car. Eventually, the door fell flush with the threshold, found its jamb, and sealed her in the echoic staircase.

Ethan leaned forward and kissed her. His kiss was hard. His tongue pushed and prodded into her lower teeth and gums. She couldn't remember the last time she'd been kissed in this fashion, with profuse desire concentrated on the lips. Kissing was a part of *trying*, but more so an act of convention rather than romance. She grew lightheaded and gripped the back of Ethan's shirt. Her mind steadied. The anticipation of it all was overwhelming, but the act, the simple act of kissing, was easier than expected.

They continued up the stairs. The light was strong, and Carissa noticed their two shadows blending on the wall, their dark forms swelling into one another. She leaned back and let a sliver of air breathe between their forms.

***

110

The room will be sterile, white, and the light harsh. Carissa will take a seat on the exam table, hearing the thin paper crinkle under her body. Jim will plop in a plastic chair that has held many men. On the wall will rest a painting of a little blond boy running through tall grass.

***

Ethan slid his key into the lock, worked the knob, and Carissa entered a bare living room—a TV in one corner and a dusty ficus in another. The overhead light consisted of three bulbs, one of which had burned out, and the refrigerator on the other side of the room grumbled. There was a book on the floor, *Facing the Music*, and Carissa was surprised by the room's emptiness. "Going for that Buddhist thing?" she said.

"Just don't spend much time here. Too busy." He kicked the book out of the way, and it knocked against the baseboard. "A drink?"

"Sure."

"Vodka and beer's all I got. What would you like?"

"Vodka's good."

"Ice?"

"Sure."

Ethan walked into the kitchen, and Carissa headed out onto the car-sized balcony. Her eyes combed over the stars and their reflection against the inky water. Planes' lights blinked as they took off from LAX, and she thought of the way Jim always called them LA's lightning bugs. Years ago, not far from here, Jim had taken her out for Valentine's Day. It was early in their relationship, and they hadn't yet tired of the forced tradition. With a stick, he'd carved "I love

111

you" in the sand, but the surf had swallowed "I love" because it was too close to the shore, leaving only "you" behind.

In time, Ethan joined Carissa on the balcony. He drank a beer, and she worked on her vodka with three ice cubes. "It's amazing how much better the world looks at night, don't you think?" he said. "Darkness covers up all the filth."

Carissa nodded.

Ethan laughed to himself, and his breath burst across the top of his beer bottle, producing a baritone hum. He slipped his arm behind Carissa, and his fingers climbed her spine until they reached her right shoulder. With his arm lifted, she could smell his deodorant—traces of pine and peppermint. She swirled the final inch of vodka around the base of her glass and put it down, letting the alcohol heat her throat as it snaked into her stomach.

***

The nurse will arrive and obtain all the vital signs. "Your heart rate's a little high," she will say. "You're probably just nervous. Just take some breaths, okay?" Carissa will breathe and breathe, feeling her heart rate slow. She will stare at the painting of the little boy running through the tall grass and wonder what it is he's searching for and whether he'll ever find it.

***

Carissa neared the bedroom, felt her feet sink into the hallway's thick maroon carpeting. Her blood pushed against her arteries, and she struggled to breathe through her nose, forcing her to drag in a breath with her mouth. When they finally reached the end of the corridor, Carissa let a breath quiver from her lips.

Ethan clicked on the light and brought the dimmer switch south. The bedroom consisted of a mattress on the floor covered in wrinkled sheets, a couple of pillows, a curtain-less window, and a poster of Hopper's *Nighthawks* tacked onto the wall with masking tape. She'd always found the painting soothing. It emitted a gritty loneliness—a couple on one side of the counter and a man, by himself, on the other end. She wondered about the lives of these subjects: What brought them to this diner in the middle of the night? Was the couple happy? Who was the desolate man? How had it happened? "We should turn the lights off, don't you think?" Carissa said, taking a seat on the edge of the bed. "You said that darkness covers up the filth."

"There's nothing filthy here," Ethan said, unlacing his shoes.

Carissa nodded. She lay on her side, with her face resting against her palm, inspecting Ethan. She heard each wingtip plop against the carpet before Ethan joined her, contouring himself to her form and kissing her, softly at first and just on the lips, then moving up to her left ear, where he blew hot breath over her lobe. Carissa rolled onto her back. Her eyes peeled on the yellow light above her. She thought she heard her phone chime. It was certainly Jim.

The first time they'd made love was on June eighth toward the end of their senior year. There had been a density to the heat, and both of them had skipped school, told their families they weren't feeling well, waited for their parents to leave for work, and met up at nearby Abalone Cove, a little bay that was never busy because of the hellish walk to the water. Signs warning of rattlesnakes were planted every

113

twenty feet, and a recent mudslide had erased the lower third of the trail. Jim kept referring to them as Lewis and Clark, and she remembered telling him not to bring history class to the beach. Once they arrived, though, they agreed it had been worth the trek. Surf pounded the shore, traced the sand, and flooded the tide pools. Carissa remembered closing her eyes and seeing the sun beat on her eyelids and savoring the clatter and grind of stones as the ebb slithered back to its home. Flies had buzzed from heaps of dried algae, and bottles had clinked in Jim's backpack. When they'd reached the opposite end of the cove, Jim had fanned out three towels—one blue, two red—and smoothed them repeatedly. "Are you ready?" he'd asked. She remembered how good it was, how he'd kept pausing and staring into her eyes, asking her whether he should keep going. It hadn't lasted long—sixty-four waves—and afterward, they had lain there, baking in the sun.

Ethan was at her neck now, licking round her throbbing jugular. He pushed her arms above her head and peeled off her sweater, showcasing her flat, cold stomach coated with goosebumps. Carissa bit her lip hard. Ethan unfastened the button, dragged down the zipper, and tossed her skirt aside. Cool air found her thighs. Ethan remained focused on her legs, brushing her flesh and stroking her calves. With each caress, Carissa drifted off, eventually turning her head away from the overhead light and sinking her face into a pillow that smelled strongly of pine.

***

"The doctor will be right in," the nurse will say. Jim will scoot his chair over to the side of the exam table and kiss Carissa on her dangling hand. The overhead

114

light will beam, and Carissa will think of the sun, that day at Abalone Cove, and the yellow glow of Ethan's bedroom. "We're finally here," Jim will say.

***

Ethan reached under the bed and removed a condom from a red wrapper. Carissa drew a breath and gulped. She brought her fingers to Ethan's chest and splayed them, moved her hands north, and felt his hair lift and bend. "Sorry," he muttered. "I can't ever seem to get these things to work. Guess I'm too excited or something." He flung the condom to the ground and reached back under the bed for another.

Carissa laughed nervously. On the bed with Ethan, she compartmentalized and didn't let her mind reel to the past or future. Her world was Ethan's bedroom—small, basic, and uncluttered.

He apologized a few more times, and she noticed thick beads of sweat on his brow glitter under the yellow light. "Are you nervous?" she asked. Ethan didn't answer. Then he nodded. "Don't be," she said, though she was happy he was. All those days she didn't feel attractive or wanted—it was nice to know she could make a young man shake. "Go ahead," Carissa said, aligning her hips with his.

Ethan slid in. He moaned.

She tugged his head to her face and tasted the humidity of his breath as he exhaled near her mouth. She wrapped her shaven legs around his back as he twisted his pelvis against hers. "Carissa," Ethan said. "Carissa." The burn of the light was strong, but she didn't shut her eyes; she allowed the rays to sting her pupils and irises and cause her eyes to water. She ran a hand along the back of his head that was slick with sweat. Her other hand found itself atop his back, and she traced her fingers through the peaks and valleys of his spine. Ethan angled her face toward his and kissed her. The grit of his stubble grated her cheeks. They locked eyes. Perspiration traced the outer rim of his face, and his smile was wide, his teeth shining. She kissed back, pulling hard on his lips. Their kisses were wet and sloppy. Drool flowed over her chin, down her throat, and pooled in the hollow of her neck. She yanked his body against hers, dug her nails into his shoulder blades, and tightened her thighs around his waist.

***

Dr. Michalski will finally enter, carrying a clipboard, and clicking a pen. He won't make eye contact with Jim or Carissa until he's been in the room for a few seconds. "So," he'll say, "your first prenatal appointment. You guys must be excited. I was on the horn with your family doctor, and he was telling me how hard you guys tried. How hard it was for you both, and how you kept at it despite all the statistics. What's meant to be is meant to be, right? So this is the longest appointment of the bunch. We're just going to run some tests, make sure everything's in order. So eleven weeks . . ." he'll say.

***

Ethan gave Carissa quick thrusts, causing her to orgasm. The feeling was so foreign that, at first, she thought something was wrong but then savored the quiver of her legs and stutter of her breath. A droplet of sweat ran down her stomach, tickling her as it encountered drier skin. Their bodies remained coiled for a few seconds, sticky.

116

He rolled over, and for the first time in a while, Carissa felt coolness slide over her body. She'd been draped by Ethan for so long that her skin itched without him on top of her. They lay still atop the damp fitted sheet. The other covers were tangled together at the foot of the bed in a mound. She tried to bring one of the sheets out to cover herself, but it didn't budge, so she sank back down, studying the light and seeing the pointed rays beam from the filament. Ethan slithered his arm behind her and pulled her toward him. She rested her head on his damp chest and listened to his heart thump.

***

Dr. Michalski will go through the routine: Ask about health details, menstrual cycles, medications, allergies, past surgeries, smoking, drinking. "Tell me about your families' medical histories," he'll say. He will run a thorough physical, a pelvic exam, then a Pap smear. "She's been vomiting *a lot*," Jim will say. The doctor will squint his eyes and look concerned. "Hmm," he'll say. After some time, he'll snap off his gloves and drop them in the trash. He'll congratulate them once more. "See you both in a bit. Just schedule your next appointment up front." Carissa will watch the doctor file down the hall and pop into another room and think he's a version of Santa Claus, spreading cheer with a clipboard and a cheap pen.

***

Carissa's white panties rested at the base of the bed, along with her purple bra. She stood tall while Ethan lolled on the mattress, his hands behind his head, watching her every move. When her bra was fastened,

117

she blotted her brow with her skirt. "Do you want something to drink?" Ethan asked.

"No," she said. "I'm fine."

"Okay," he said. He hopped out of bed. A spring inside the mattress snapped, and she studied Ethan as he left the room nude, his leg muscles taking turns tightening and relaxing as he strolled away.

After putting on the rest of her clothes, she adjusted the straps of her heels, threw her purse over her shoulder, and headed down the hallway. She could still feel Ethan between her thighs, his essence seeping from her body. "Goodbye, Ethan," she said.

"Oh, wow," he said. "So soon?" He scooted behind the open refrigerator door. The sharp light spread over his hips and stomach. He undid the top of a bottle of orange juice and took a swig. Carissa inspected his body, noticing a scar on the right side of his chest. "Do you have my phone number?" he asked. "Do I have yours?"

"Yes," she said.

Ethan scurried over to her, naked. He brought her against him. His scent was so strong that even when she breathed through her mouth, she could seemingly taste the pine smell. Her pointer finger migrated to his lower back, and she let it sink into one of the dimples at the base of his spine. "Let's do this again, okay?" he said.

"Okay." She nodded, let herself out, and hurried down the stairwell. Once she reached the street, she drew in a deep breath. Everything was fine. That was the beauty about being a good person—when you did something other than decent, no one would believe it.

The vinyl in her Pontiac was cold, so she blasted the heat and felt the warmth graze her face. She plucked her phone from her purse. Jim had texted twice: "Go get 'em!" in the first message, and

"Thinking of you. XOXO . . ." in the second. She opened her eyes wide, flipped down the visor mirror, and checked her face: her neck was red despite her chill, and her lipstick had lightened from red to rose. She plucked her car key from her purse and rammed it into the ignition.

***

They will schedule another appointment with Dr. Michalski and be back in a few weeks. The secretary will smile and hand them a little card with the time and date of their next meeting. She will tell them to call and cancel if there's any problem and to let them know if anything should pop up—any questions or concerns. Carissa and Jim will take to the hall and walk away from the office. "Oh, my God," Jim will say, pulling Carissa's body close to his. "Can you believe it? It all happened so fast, right? Can I drive you home?" he will ask. She will remind him that they each drove their own cars to the office, but he will insist. "Screw it," he'll say. "I'll come pick it up later. I want to be with *you*—and my kid. The three of us. One big ol' happy family." Carissa will smile and bring herself to kiss Jim on the cheek.

***

Carissa drove home quickly. When she arrived at her place, Jim rushed to the door. "Hey," he said. "I texted you a couple of times. How'd everything go? You look kind of sick. You okay?"

"I'm totally fine. It was really cold at his house, or maybe I was nervous or something, so as soon as I got in the car, I cranked the heater." She was calm, did everything as she normally did, kicked off her shoes and hung her purse up on a hook in the foyer. She was amazed at how easily moral fiber could be stretched. Would it snap back like a rubber band or remain elongated like a piece of gum?

Jim wore his reading glasses on the tip of his nose and had the "Calendar" section of the newspaper rolled up tight. His head craned from side to side. "Trying to kill a damn fly," he said. "It's been buzzing and buzzing and landing on the TV and giving everyone moles in strange places."

Carissa headed to the faucet and filled a glass with water.

"So how'd it go?" he asked. "Does he like you?"

The glass overflowed. She shut off the tap. "Yes," she said. "I think he does."

"Of course he does. It'd be impossible not to. Did he offer you anything?"

She pulled a loose strand of fabric from her skirt and ripped it off in a clean motion. "Nothing formal, but I know he's interested."

"This is great news," Jim said. He came into the kitchen and also filled up a glass of water. He lifted his glass above his head. "So happy for you," he said. "So tonight? What do you think? Are you up for it? Is it a good time?"

Carissa tilted her glass back and swallowed as much water as she could.

***

Their footsteps will echo through the parking garage as they hold hands and make their way toward Carissa's Pontiac. Once inside the car, music will jump from the speakers, and Jim will turn the volume down. "Aren't you glad we didn't give up? That we kept at it? That we're a real family now? My dad said it's a miracle, but I told him it's just what was meant to be. The three of us—a triangle, a tripod, a whatever."

Carissa will buckle her seatbelt and turn the radio back up a little. She'll know that Jim will want her to say more, but all she'll say is yes. As they drive away from the medical building, she'll check her email, and see a message from Ethan. "Just thinking of you," it will say. "Been a while. Hope to see you soon." She will open her window all the way and wish for more air to rush over her face. "It was so worth it, that's all. Don't you think?" Jim will say. And Carissa will sit there, still, see the green traffic light ahead switch to yellow, and listen to the motor slow down as they come to a stop. "You have something—someone, rather—inside of you. Isn't that beautiful?" Jim will say.

In time, the light will turn green. The car will speed up. Carissa will nod and seek comfort behind closed eyes. She will feel the wind swell and wrap her hands around her belly, wishing she didn't feel so separate from what was growing inside of her.

121

A LITTLE OFF THE TOP

Shaker stood in the barbershop alone. He was new in town, and the other barber, the owner of the shop, had given him the late shift—from two to nine p.m. He didn't understand why she stayed open so late in this small coastal town where the homes went dark after dinnertime, but he had work, and that was all that mattered.

It was quarter after eight, but since night arrived early these November days, Shaker thought it seemed much later. No one would show up for a haircut at this time. No one had yesterday or the day before, so he started cleaning up. He dunked his combs in the blue Barbicide, organized his brushes, and filled his spray bottle. Then he clicked off the red-white-and-blue barbershop pole.

He plopped down on his chair and placed his feet against the metal footrest. There wasn't a more comfortable chair in the world, and Shaker didn't understand why the manufacturer hadn't made designs for homes and offices.

Rain fell harder now. Since he had arrived in Point Reyes, it had rained almost every day. The big surprise was when it was clear. He clicked on the TV and watched a college football game, Fresno State versus USC. He didn't care who won. To him, they were all winners: all that fame and all those dreams ahead of them, and they weren't even old enough to buy beer.

The handle turned, and the door squeaked open. A man took a step inside. He was small, wearing a heavy coat, scarf, and a black fedora with the brim pulled low.

"Oh," Shaker said. "Um, we're closed."

"Why are you still here, then?" the man said in a smoker's voice.

"Just cleaning up."

The man entered and closed the door behind him. He worked his arms free from his coat and secured it to the rack by the entrance. Then he tossed his fedora onto a chair in the waiting area. The short man was old, maybe eighty. He wore a thin gray mustache and tortoiseshell glasses that sat on the bridge of his nose. Wiry hairs sprouted from his ears, too.

"You're in my seat," the old man said.

Shaker sighed, got off the chair, and went to press Power on the remote control.

"Leave it on," the man said.

"All right," Shaker said. "Have a seat."

The man had trouble getting into the chair but eventually settled in. Once seated, Shaker pumped the pedal and raised the old man into the air. He then secured a neck strip to the man's nape and draped a barber's cape around his torso.

"I love these chairs," the man said.

"I know, right?" Shaker misted the man's hair with the spray bottle. The man's hair provided little coverage on the top of his head, but the sides and back were thick and wavy. "So, what can I do for you today?"

The man coughed, then said, "Cut the back and sides short. And only a little off the top. Trying to grow it out."

Shaker continued to spray, and the old man shut his eyes and let the droplets greet his face.

"Always feels nice," the man said.

Shaker glanced at his watch. It was twenty till nine. He reached for his scissors and comb and began at the back of the man's head.

"Who do you like?" the man asked, pointing to the TV.

"Fresno, I guess."

"They're good this year."

"Yeah?"

"Yes."

A car outside drove too fast down the road, and the tires sloshed on the wet pavement.

"Never seen you here before. You just move or something?" the man said.

"Yeah, not that long ago," Shaker said, taking a few strands of the man's hair between his fingers.

"How do you like it?"

"It's nice. Quiet."

"Yes, too quiet sometimes."

"Yeah. And a little cold for me. I'm from Palm Springs, so even hell's cold."

"Nice out there, though." The man folded his hands and lined his gaze with the entrance. Rain beads traced the windows and rapped on the roof. "I'm Horace," the man said.

"Shaker."

The two men nodded.

"What kind of a name is Shaker? And for a barber? Dangerous." Horace coughed again. This one lasted a bit.

"You all right?"

"Yes. It's just damp, you know? Are you married?"

"No," Shaker said. He dropped his comb to the floor and pulled a new one from the Barbicide. It was the first time someone had asked him that question since he'd tried to start over, and he pictured Allison

125

on his bed, her hair wild on the pillows and her shirt hiked up past her belly button.

"What a catch," Horace said. "Did you see that? With one hand!"

"Yes, what a beauty," Shaker said, pulling a comb through Horace's shiny hair. "How about you . . . You married?"

Horace took his time to answer. He flicked a few wet chunks of his hair off the black barber's cape, and they landed on the floor without a sound. "Yes, been happily married for over fifty years. Met her at a funeral of all places. She's home right now making meatloaf. She really makes a terrific meatloaf. You know what she does to make it so good?"

Shaker didn't answer, figuring the question to be rhetorical, but Horace craned his neck and stared at him, wanting a reply.

"What?" Shaker said, swapping his scissors for thinning shears.

"She soaks little pieces of bread in milk for a few hours . . . then sprinkles them throughout the loaf. Stays moist that way. You like meatloaf?"

"Sure. Reminds me of when I was a kid." Shaker thought back to those nights at the table when his father would come home from work as a police officer, full of brave stories, his uniform still crisp after the long day. He'd always hoped he'd be a hero to someone the way his dad was to him.

"You need those little pieces of bread."

Shaker nodded and snipped around the arches of Horace's ears. Four times he'd failed the firefighter entrance exam. He just wasn't fast or strong enough. The worst part wasn't learning that he hadn't made the cut but coming home to Allison and her pity-glazed eyes.

"Kids?" Horace asked.

126

The volume on the TV surged as Fresno State's quarterback fumbled the snap.

"No," Shaker said. "You?"

"Yes, two boys. They're both doctors now. One's in Seattle, the other's outside of Austin." He coughed. Once it cleared, he continued. "Just had my first grandchild, too, a sweet little boy. They named him Horace."

Shaker couldn't picture a little kid named Horace. Would he carry a cane to preschool or push a walker with tennis balls secured to the ends of its legs?

Allison had wanted children at one point, but like many things, they hadn't materialized.

Each time Horace spoke about his wife or children or grandchildren or famous bread-soaked meatloaf, his voice softened. It was as if normal conversation was a pair of grease-soaked coveralls, while his family was a white-tie affair. When Shaker looked at Horace, he didn't see a man in love. He didn't see his father who brought his mother flowers for no other reason than to celebrate a Tuesday in June. His father had always told Shaker that he'd grow up strong and smart and kind, but he hadn't. And Shaker believed that who you were at forty was who you were at fifty and sixty. The last time—the fourth time—that he had failed the firefighter's exam, he'd met another dejected man in the parking lot. They'd sat in the man's car, bitching, puffing weed, and slugging beers—a couple of forty-year-old teenagers.

"My sons' wives don't cook like mine, though," Horace said. "Today's women don't know how to cook. No. The only things they can make are reservations. I bet if you open the door, you can smell the meatloaf. I live just up the road. We've been there a long time, but we met during the summer of '48 in Cincinnati, at a ballgame."

127

"Oh, that's cool." Shaker thought Horace had said that he'd met his wife at a funeral, but he didn't stop him.

"Yes, we were at the ballpark, and she was sitting in the same section as me. After the third inning, she hurried up the steps and returned sometime later with a bucket of popcorn. You should've seen the size of the bucket. Just as she made it to her row, she tripped and spilled it all, and I rushed over to help her. Oh, was she embarrassed . . . Her face was as red as the uniforms."

USC kicked a field goal and knotted the game up at ten. Shaker reached for the clippers and evened out Horace's neckline while the old man went on and on about the bright lights of the stadium and what his wife smelled like that summer night and how her hands were shiny with butter.

"Do you want to see a photo of her?" he asked.

"All right," Shaker said, pulling his clippers away from Horace's head. Horace leaned forward, flung the cape to his side, and eventually yanked his brown wallet from his back pocket. It was thick, crammed with coupons and cards and pieces of yellow paper. "Damn, you got a yard sale living in your pants."

"What?" Horace said.

Shaker didn't answer.

Horace spread apart the billfold. Everything but cash seemed to live inside. He searched for the photo, then grabbed it, unfolded it, placed it on his knee, and worked the creases out with his liver-spotted hand. He held it high. "This was taken a few years after we met . . . at a friend's party in Dallas." The woman in the photo looked familiar—a dirty blonde with dark-red lipstick. Shaker thought he'd seen her on TV before, advertising an energy drink. The edges of the

128

photo were jagged and the paper shiny, as if it had been torn from a magazine. Wouldn't a picture from that time have been in black and white?

"Gorgeous, right?" Horace said, placing the crinkled woman back in his wallet, and the wallet back in his trousers.

"You're a lucky man," Shaker said.

Horace nodded.

The woman in the photo looked nothing like Allison, except for the large smile. That night, after another unsuccessful try at the station, she'd glared and yelled at Shaker for being high and drunk. She'd called him a loser and told him to just work as a barber. "Stop trying to be *the man*, and just be *a man*," she'd said. Without thinking, he'd grabbed a plate wrapped with tinfoil on the dinner table and hurled it her way. He'd felt the relationship die right then, and he turned from the kitchen, with Allison clutching her forehead, and took to the front door.

Horace clapped his hands as Fresno State ran the ball for a first down. "What a spin," he said. "You always been a barber?"

"Pretty much. And you? What did you do?"

"I was an architect. Ever been to Indianapolis?"

"No."

"Designed a lot of churches out there . . . a lot of commercial buildings, too."

"And your wife?"

"She took care of the kids. Boys don't grow up to be lawyers without someone working the levers."

Shaker shut off the trimmer and yanked the hair dryer free from its holster. He blew hot air over Horace's head, allowing stray hairs to fly from his scalp. Horace closed his eyes, and his lips curved in a smile as the warm stream tickled his brow, crown, neck, and ears.

"Oh, that feels good," Horace said. "It's been so cold."

Shaker remembered shaving alongside Allison in their bathroom, where she'd swing her hairdryer around wildly, trying to dry and style her thick mane. He, too, had always savored the heat of her stray gusts, and it was one of many memories that he'd needed to power through those homeless nights at the park, under glittering stars and atop heavy cardboard.

Shaker shook some talcum powder onto a shaving brush and dusted Horace's neck and ears.

"That's nice," Horace said. "Smells soft, like youth."

Fresno State flung a pass and entered the red zone. Shaker handed Horace a hand mirror and had him hold it up to the right side of his face and angle it so that he could see his neckline in the wall-mounted mirror.

"Clean and tapered," Shaker said.

"Yes, perfect."

"You want some hair tonic?"

"That's all right. At this age, it's best not to call attention to your head. Plus, my wife likes it natural."

Shaker ran his fingers through Horace's hair one last time, then unfastened the neck strip, and yanked off the cape. Usually, people were eager to jump out of the chair and take off, especially late at night, but Horace stayed put. He scratched at his scalp and crossed his legs. "It's gonna be a close one all the way," he said. "Tit for tat, tit for tat."

The gutter over the entryway was filling up and overflowing, and each time a car drove by, its headlights lit up thick strands of water. "It's good and warm in here," Horace said. Shaker agreed. He remembered the surprising cold of Palm Springs during the winter, and how there were times when he'd trembled with hunger and begged to die and be reunited with his parents, but not long after, a spot opened up at the shelter, and he met the owner of the shop's brother, a preacher, while eating supper. "Move up north, son. My sister could use a good barber. It's not too late," he'd said.

Horace removed his glasses and cleaned them with the sleeve of his sweater, then coughed a few times, and Shaker patted his back.

"Okay," Shaker said, "you're all set." He stomped the pedal, brought the chair to its lowest level, extended his arm, and helped Horace down. "It's fifteen bucks."

Horace reached for his wallet and pried open the tough leather. He removed four folded bills—a ten, a five, two singles—and handed them over. A couple scraps of paper fluttered to the floor, but Horace didn't notice, and Shaker didn't care to mention it.

"I'll see you soon," Horace said, pushing his glasses up. He plopped on his fedora and grabbed his overcoat. Shaker walked over to the door and held the coat open so that Horace could easily thread his arms through the sleeves.

"Button up," Shaker said. "It's really coming down."

"Yes," Horace said. "I'm just looking forward to that meatloaf."

Shaker nodded and smiled and felt pressure in his chest.

"I'm so hungry for it." Horace opened the door, and the rush of rain found their ears. "There . . . you can almost smell it, right? All those spices." He tilted his head back, shut his eyes, and inhaled through his nose.

Shaker popped his head out the door and did the same. "Yes. It's a beautiful smell."

Horace tipped the bill of his hat, buttoned his coat, and turned up his lapels. He headed off, down the street, through the rain, his body blending with the night one step at a time.

In minutes, Shaker figured, Horace would be back at his home, where he'd change into his robe and cook eggs or noodles with his socks pulled up to his shins. Maybe he'd watch a game show or enjoy a movie and fall asleep on his recliner. Or maybe he'd just listen to the rain and wonder when morning would come.

Shaker closed the door, grabbed his broom, and swept Horace's hair into a pile. All white except for those two pieces of paper that had escaped from his wallet. Shaker bent down and picked them up. They were again from a magazine—one a portrait of a redhead with her fingers placed coyly over her mouth, the other an action shot of a boy playing tennis. Shaker studied the photos over and over again before sliding them into his pocket. He continued to sweep the floor, the roaring sound of the football crowd echoing through the empty barbershop.

ON THE ODOMETER

I

At 18,000 miles, when my hair was still blondish, Dad flung me the keys to the '53 DeSoto Powermaster. It was a voluptuous sedan, with a heavy chrome grille, painted in a deep red color that Dad called "Sophia Loren's lipstick." I was fifteen. It was a Sunday, and we were still wearing our suits from church. I didn't know why he'd done it since the car was only a few years old, but it was my first ride, and I worked that beast all over Peoria—up and down the same streets—counting how many green lights I could rush through without finding a red one.

II

Somewhere along I-55, we hit 22,000 miles. Mom and Dad and me and Ricky were headed to St. Louis to catch the World Series. The DeSoto had never left Illinois, but it held up well, even in the cold, even with Ricky leaning over the front seat and messing with the radio. When Mom had to use the restroom, I pulled off around Springfield into a drive-in called, I think, the Cozy Dog. Dad popped out and lit a smoke, and I watched him brush off bits of ash that settled on his tie.

III

29,000 came just before I left for Purdue. Mom and Dad and Ricky helped me stuff the DeSoto, and Mom kept saying to call her when I got there, let her know that I'd arrived safe and sound, and to fill her in on what my dorm room looked like. Dad kept telling her that it would look just like any other dorm room, and I kept agreeing with him, but still, she insisted, and for some reason, so did Ricky. I didn't get too close to them. I knew all it would take was someone's hand on my shoulder or a simple "Love you." Ricky saluted me, his fingers tight and pressed against his temple. And I was off, out the driveway, the whitewalls gripping the road, onward to West Lafayette to become a Boilermaker, whatever that was.

IV
At 33,000, I returned home for winter break. Christine, my girlfriend, came for a few days, too, and Mom finally had a houseguest worthy of the fancy soaps and towels she'd collected for years. I was a junior; Christine was a sophomore. I studied architecture, while Christine pursued finance. Mom had aged, her hair grayer, and for the first time, she looked old— with her stubby eyelashes and veiny hands. Dad seemed the same, though. His glasses just kept getting bigger. Ricky was a senior in high school, and he showed me his letterman jacket, even let me try it on. The fire popped, and Dad threw on another log. Mom kept swinging her eyes over Christine—up and down, studying the golden dove brooch I'd given her.

V
I married Christine at 40,000 miles in Evanston, Illinois—her hometown—at St. Mary's on a Sunday in November. The time felt right—we'd grown enough but needed to grow some more. Mom had told me that she loved Christine, particularly the way she gazed at me as if I could solve anything. Ricky got along well with her, too. She told him how women liked to be treated and to stop wearing ball caps everywhere, and he obliged, took it in, while most likely daydreaming about curveballs and splitters. After the sacrament, we were sprinkled with rice en route to the DeSoto. I

135

opened the car door for Christine, helped her with her train, and then whipped around to my side. We drove off with rice pelting the roof and aluminum cans bouncing and popping behind the Powermaster. Christine clutched my fingers, and I glanced in the rearview, brushing over all those cheering and clapping people on the church steps.

VI

44,000 came fast. Christine and I moved to Indianapolis. She got a job at a local bank, and I started at an architectural firm. We bought a house, a three-bedroom, at the end of a cul-de-sac. The place was yellow with navy shutters, and apple trees dotted the front yard in a diamond-like formation that seemed perfect for a hassle-free game of baseball.

VII

The DeSoto served us well at 46,000 miles. Its trunk could've *also* swallowed Jonah, so it was good for Saturday garage-sale trips. Christine sat in the passenger seat with the newspaper in one hand and a map in the other, calling out, "Right," and "Left," and "Straight ahead." We crammed the Powermaster full of furniture, and slowly, week by week, filled each room with dressers and beds and nightstands till the house looked like Mom and Dad's, till echoes no longer bounced around the floor plan. Each night, it seemed as if Christine and I were playing house. We could turn the heat up as high as we wanted. We could stay up late. We could make love and pot roast.

VIII

At 53,000, Christine gave birth to Julia. I got ahead of myself and baby-proofed the sockets, toilets, and swiped knickknacks into boxes. I built a tree house and even roped an old whitewall to the oak in the backyard—all that for a girl who didn't yet have a laugh. We used the DeSoto less, and most weeks, it sat in the garage, under a blanket, waiting for Sundays and holidays. I found rust on the bumper, too, even though I'd always done as Dad had said and washed the rock salt off as soon as I got home.

IX
60,000 was easy to remember because Mom got sick, lung cancer. She'd never smoked, but she had taken in a lot of Dad's fumes. She never complained or talked about it. All the information came from Dad, quietly, quickly, over the phone or when she was in some distant part of the house. Ricky took her shopping a lot, said she seemed happy trying on clothes and buying outfits. A few times a month, she got her hair done, too—"a permanent," she called it. Ricky joked that if it was, in fact, "permanent," the upkeep shouldn't have been so demanding. Whenever I'd get a job in Illinois, I'd stay with my parents, and Ricky would come over. Since Mom was tired, I'd make omelets with Dad. We'd make Ricky's really spicy and watch him try to be macho. "It's not too bad. Really. It's not bad at all," he'd say, his face redder than brake lights. Mom would laugh and laugh.

X
There was a night at 64,000, when we'd just finished dinner, and Mom wanted ice cream. We piled in the DeSoto, and Dad caught my negligence, pointed out patches of leather that were cracking and beginning to rip. He told me I should've splurged for better tires. We grabbed some ice cream at Outlaw's, which I thought seemed like a strange name for a place that dealt with sprinkles for a living, but the product was

creamy and so cold, and we all sat there in the DeSoto, under yellow streetlights, with the radio soft, licking our chocolate cones.

XI

Julia really got into art somewhere around 72,000. She especially enjoyed drawing trees. Christine always felt like staying in, having some time to herself, so Julia and I took off, wended through back roads, and stopped whenever she found an oak or pine with tormented branches. The bench seat was perfect, too, because I'd drive with Julia pressed right up against me, even swing my arm around her when the road straightened out. While she sketched, I closed my eyes and listened to a radio station that loved crooners. Perry Como leaked through, and I thought the DeSoto was at peace, piping in tunes from its generation.

XII

At 79,000, Ricky was over playing HORSE with Julia in the driveway. Christine and I were inside, cleaning up after a dinner party. I wanted to touch her but thought maybe she didn't want me to. I was scared to ask her about it, and then, hours later, after Ricky and Julia headed to the mall to buy some softball gear, she said she was unhappy and didn't love her life. There was a day, she said, when she got into her car and started to drive off. I told her to stay, and she said she would. I touched her fingers and felt her nails dig into my palm.

XIII

Mom died at 88,000. I'd been over at the house the week before, and she'd been dressed up real nice, all in turquoise with a black hat, as if she were headed to the Kentucky Derby. She'd even wanted to go for a walk, but it was cold, so we only made it down the block. She was quiet, and whenever I glanced her way, she smiled with only her lips. "A blue jay," she said. "A blue jay." Every bird she spotted was a blue jay, and I didn't say otherwise.

XIV

Somewhere around 93,000, when Dad was seventy-six, we moved him into a retirement home not far from our place. Living alone didn't work for him any longer: He slept until noon, and a couple times I got calls from neighbors saying that he'd left the front door wide open for hours, days even, in the middle of winter. The doctors had fancy words for what was happening to his brain, but all I knew was that he started calling me Joseph, like the brother he'd lost in the war.

XV

At 96,000, despite Christine and I attending therapy, going to Mass, and joining a nature club (per the advice of the counselor), she told me she wanted a divorce. It was a Monday afternoon. I was at my drafting table, designing the entryway of an apartment complex. Her blouse was buttoned incorrectly, and a few inked notes were scrawled on her hand: dry cleaning, checks, and something else I couldn't read. I was glad my mother wasn't alive to hear the news and relieved my father wouldn't be able to understand it. Part of me wanted to fight for Christine, but I knew that matters of love didn't need the approval of both partners—that this wasn't the usual swimming pool or ski trip discussion. "We'll tell Julia when she gets home from school, okay? She probably feels it coming. She's been smarter than us for a while now." I nodded, and Christine let me know she was going for a walk. I tried to leave my desk but couldn't. My legs were numb. I reached for my ruler and pressed on, detailing the ramp for wheelchair access. Thirty minutes later, the phone rang. Christine had been found in the road. She'd struck her head on the side of a curb and wasn't responding.

XVI
At 97,000, Christine was finally released. She'd spent four months in the hospital in a coma, and the doctors had performed two brain surgeries. She'd never again be my Purdue Christine, the one who drank Coke for breakfast and refused to write in anything but red ink. She was alive, but most likely would never walk or talk again. To my surprise, I enjoyed bathing her each morning, bringing her to the tub, and running the soap over her rounded ankles. She didn't smile, but her eyes grew large, and she blinked often, and I thought of it as our form of Morse code.

XVII
99,000 happened on our way to the creek. Me, Julia, and Christine sat up front on the bench seat, and Ricky took care of Dad in the back. When we got there, Ricky and Julia fished, while Christine, Dad, and I caught rays of sun on our faces. I thought Dad could make out the DeSoto. I thought he was happy to see the red beast at (almost) capacity, heavy with people, and he ran his fingers over the chrome handles and sweeping fenders. "Beautiful, beautiful," he said.

XVIII
The engine hit the 100,000 mark on the second of July. Julia and I wanted the milestone to happen on Independence Day, but we had to take a detour one morning, and the DeSoto tacked on a few extra miles. We cheered, though, and Julia kissed her mother. "Pull

over, Dad," she said. "I want to look at the moon." She told me she'd read something in the paper about a supermoon. She rushed out and took in the sky, and I aided Christine. The night seemed the same as the one before it. "Maybe I got the date wrong," Julia said. But we stayed there anyway, running our eyes over the normal moon and normal stars, with several planes blinking and passing each other in the night, forming a sort of ephemeral constellation.

XIX

At 106,000, Julia enlisted in the Army. I'd always thought it was a bad idea for Dad to tell her all those war stories, because I saw the way her gaze narrowed and her attention span grew. Ricky's face had done the same thing whenever anyone spoke about Stan Musial. "I'll come home often," she said. "And you can always drive down to North Carolina. It's not *that* far. It's nice there, warmer, and a lot closer to the ocean. Imagine the fish we can catch there."

XX

When the DeSoto collected its 108,000th mile, hospice took over for Dad. I sat by his bedside, my hands resting on his knee. He hadn't been shaved in some time, and light white whiskers had formed under his sideburns. I'd never seen him unshaven except for that one month when Ricky and I were boys and had given him the chickenpox. He couldn't shave then, because he had a sizable rash around his lips, so he grew a beard that Mom made him get rid of as soon as he got well. "That's not the man I married. You look like Castro," she kept saying. Even in that sterile room, with little to smile about, I managed. I stroked my forefinger against the grain of his beard. I did it for minutes, savoring the warmth of his face and the bend of his sharp hairs. It had been a long time since I'd kissed Dad. After I'd gone to college, we started hugging; later, we shook hands and patted each other on the back, like jocks. So I hunched over and pecked his cheek. His scent was strong—a mix of cologne and night sweat—and I brought my lips to his soft skin again. And again. In his bed, like this, he was quiet and strong; he was the same Godlike man I'd worshipped as a boy, from the doorway, when I would get up early to watch cartoons with Ricky and study the rising and falling of his chest.

XXI

At 109,000, Ricky, Julia, Christine, and I watched the Super Bowl. Julia was home for a week and seemed okay. She fed her mother, and it brought me back to Christine making her own baby food for Julia. She didn't trust "company" baby food, so she bought her own produce—mostly carrots and squash—and puréed them daily. Now, during the million-dollar commercials of the big game, Julia returned the favor, brought spoonfuls to her mother's mouth, minus the airplane noises. Ricky's then-girlfriend, Sam, had seen the DeSoto when she'd pulled up and asked me if she could take it for a spin. Since the game was a blowout, I brought it out and allowed Sam to drive the Powermaster. Ricky sat in the passenger seat, and I took to the back for the first time since "parking" with Christine at Purdue. I was young again on the rear bench seat. I put the window down, felt the rush. I was nine and ready for basketball at recess. I was twelve and bundled for hunting season. I was fourteen and dressed for the Strangers in the Night Dance. Sam laughed as she drove. "It's so smooth," she kept saying. "The engine sounds so good," she kept saying. "Why

don't they make cars like this any longer?" she kept
saying.

XXII

By the time 110,000 rolled around, Christine and I had
a steadfast routine. Each day began with breakfast for
the both of us at a nearby diner followed by eight a.m.
Mass. We'd arrive at quarter till and sit in the back. I'd
wrap her in my arms, and she'd stay pressed against
my side, never drifting away. I'd grip my rosary beads,
and Father Raymond would come by during
communion and hand-deliver a Host to Christine's
mouth. Occasionally, her tongue would slide against
Father's fingers, but he never said a word. He always
bowed his head and muttered to himself. My prayers
were fourfold: Ricky's happiness, Julia's safety,
Christine's health, and my parents' peace. Julia worried
me most. She'd been deployed to Iraq. It was
sometimes weeks before I heard her voice. I always
expected to see soldiers knocking at the door, standing
straight on the welcome mat.

XXIII

Finally, at 113,000, Julia came home. She wasn't my
little girl any longer. She was distant, only speaking
when spoken to. Her eyes were sunken, and wrinkles
had claimed her forehead. I often heard her wake up in
the middle of the night and head to the kitchen.
Sometimes, she cried. Whenever I asked her about it,
she just told me it was hard coming back and that
"reheated food never tasted the same." Ricky brought
out the Julia I knew, though. With him, she was
younger, freer. The two of them would read on the
back porch, and I would come out and struggle with
the crossword just to sit next to her.

XXIV

It was at 115,000 that Ricky got pink-slipped and
moved in with me, Christine, and Julia. I was out in the
garage, trying to figure out why the DeSoto had quit.
It had been running well. Sure, it leaked, but few cars
from Ike's first term didn't. The engine wouldn't start.
Not even the prelude to its hearty grumble. Ricky
came out and took a look, called a buddy of his from
the Y, a mechanic. When the mechanic arrived, he
plopped down on his creeper and slid under the
Powermaster. With each sweep of his flashlight, he
said, "Oh, Jesus." Ricky asked him what he was talking
about, and the man answered. "Rust," he said. "A good
amount of buildup along the undercarriage. No matter
what you do, it sneaks in. Surprised you made it this
far." I didn't say a thing. Ricky slammed the hood and
caressed the side mirror.

XXV

At 115,000, a man drove over with a flatbed truck. I'd
gotten an estimate to fix the DeSoto, but it was
expensive, silly, too, since I didn't drive it that often.
Money these days had to flow toward Christine and
Julia, who was now seeking professional help, and the
DeSoto still had some value to collectors and
hobbyists. The man with the flatbed backed down the
driveway. He wore a patchy beard and a red-and-black
Paul Bunyan shirt. I helped him with the Powermaster,
dropped the gearshift into neutral, and pushed it out
into the driveway. "The owner's real happy about the
deal you gave him," the man said. "Told me he's gonna
repaint it midnight blue and reupholster the interior.
Suede, I think he said. He's gonna enter it in car shows
every now and then, too." I nodded and felt a burn
behind my eyes. Once the DeSoto was up on the
flatbed, he shackled the wheels with heavy chains. It

was cold, and I shoved my hands deep into my pockets. "Have a good one," the man said, hopping up and into his truck, my keys jingling in his grimy hand. The air brake hissed, and the truck lurched forward. "Wait," I said.

XXVI

At 115,000, a couple days after Thanksgiving, when all the dishes were scrubbed and stacked and returned to their cupboards, the postman came to the door with a box. "Got another one, Julia," the postman said, and she thanked him, rushed into the kitchen, and followed Ricky and me to the garage. We ripped open the box, and I placed the new air pump Julia had found online alongside the other shiny parts. "Only a few more now," Ricky said. I smiled. Then, not understanding why, I climbed inside the DeSoto, turned the key, and listened to the scratchy radio. Ricky and Julia joined me on the front bench seat. I stared out the windshield at the cluttered garage wall, gripping the steering wheel, my fingers deep in the grooves.

I drifted back to I-55, heading south, flying fast, with all those miles to go.

LA JOLLA

They were getting ready for bed. Jay stood in front of his sink, and Amber in front of hers. Some days, Amber thought, sleep was more deserved than others, and today—tonight, rather—was one of those.

"Everything all right?" Jay asked. "You've been quiet for a while." He worked his toothbrush over his front teeth.

Amber brought her eyes over to meet his in the center of the mirror. "Yes," she said. "Think I'm just tired." She applied some night cream to her face, working the lotion into her skin in tight circles.

"I know. What a day," he said. "I'm beat. You were right: we probably should've just stayed in San Diego for the night. The drive didn't seem that bad going, but twice in one day is a lot."

"Yeah," she said.

Jay slapped a little cologne onto his neck. He did this every night. Amber liked it, too. She found it comforting to pick up on traces of citrus when she rolled his way in bed. In the beginning of their relationship, she thought it was strange that each evening Jay took a long time getting ready for bed. He showered and scrubbed, even shaved, and always applied cologne, telling her that his regimen made a lot of sense and that during the day you get dirty and you don't want to bring all that filth to bed.

"Next time, I—*we*, I mean—head down there," he said, "will be for my thirtieth reunion, right? After the twentieth comes the thirtieth . . . or is there a twenty-fifth?"

"I think it depends on the school," she said.

"And you never want to go to yours? Isn't your twentieth in a couple of years?"

"Didn't like those people back then, so I don't see why I'd like them now."

"People change, though," he said, removing his contact lenses.

"I'm not sure they do. They just learn to live better with what they have."

He nodded.

She ripped off a strand of floss.

"It's just nice to see what people have been up to, you know? I don't go down there much, and a lot of them, like Sean and Ian, have moved away."

"What about Dallas?" she said.

"Dallas . . ." he said, reaching for the bottle of blue mouthwash. "Who's Dallas? That tall guy with the Hawaiian shirt?"

"Yes," she said.

"Never knew him well. Just one of those people—not a bad guy, not a good guy, just another cloud in the sky."

Amber felt flushed, and even though she'd spent time lacquering her face with lotion, she turned on her sink's spigot and splashed her face over and over. It was cooling and fresh, and she didn't want to stop.

Jay gargled and spit. "Did he talk to you?" he asked.

"Who?"

"That guy . . . Dallas."

"A little."

"Oh," Jay said. He put on his glasses and made his way into the bedroom. Once there, he clicked on his bedside light, slid between the sheets, and started reading his book. Amber had asked him the title a few times, but she couldn't remember it at the moment.

Something about Egypt and birds and family. Yes, a bird had escaped from its cage, and the family was searching for it.

She washed her hands and filed into the bedroom. She joined Jay in bed and clicked on her light. Outside, two cats fought, sending sharp growls into the quiet air, startling both Amber and Jay. He looked up from his book, and suddenly, the noise stopped.

She reached for her sudoku magazine and got to it, scrawling possible numbers in the margins as a gentle breeze stirred their wind chime near the front door.

"Did he mention me at all? Dallas?" Jay asked.

"He just asked how you were doing. How long we'd been married."

"Oh, that's nice," he said, getting up and opening a couple windows on the far end of the bedroom. Neighborhood birds rattled off a few trills, and a car rushed by, its brakes screeching as it neared a stop sign.

***

There was a bowl of punch with shards of ice in it and blasting music: MC Hammer and New Kids on the Block and even a little Nirvana. Basically, it was a prom, Amber thought, a prom where all the guys had less hair and bigger wallets. The reunion was held in Jay's high school gymnasium with a banner that stretched the length of the basketball court. It read: WELCOME CLASS OF '93! Jay had even shown her where he'd hit the game-winner he always talked about—the spot where he'd knocked in a three from the corner to put his Titans over the top.

When Eileen, his old friend, approached and asked him to dance, Jay gazed at Amber as if asking for permission, and she smiled, opened her arms like some sort of queen, and told him to have fun. Eileen's unattractiveness made the decision an easy one.

Amber helped herself to a tall glass of punch and stayed close to the wall. A man approached. He was red-faced, sweaty, and tall—maybe six foot five with hairy hands. She'd never seen a man with such hairy hands—big tufts on his fingers. Most of the men at the reunion wore suits, but he stood solid in a Hawaiian shirt and pleated khakis.

"Are you Jay's wife?" he asked, leaning in to combat the music. He stared at Amber's nametag. "Amber Sinclair . . . as in Jay Sinclair?" His breath smelled of alcohol, and his eyes had rested on her name tag and hovered about her cleavage for far too long. "I'm Dallas," he said. "What a pretty ring you have there. A black pearl . . . look at that!"

"Yes, I'm Jay's wife," she said.

"Jay," he said, "what a guy."

"I think so," she said.

Madonna's "Vogue" bounced through the gym, and Amber watched Jay disappear in a throng of drunken men and women. He removed his blazer and whipped it around like a towel. Most of the people around him did their best to imitate Madonna's dance, framing their faces with their hands.

"Does he ever mention me?" Dallas asked.

"Yes," Amber said, even though Jay never had. She was sure she would've remembered a name like Dallas. It was her parents' favorite show. "Only good things," she said, smiling.

"That's funny," he said, a smirk on his lips.

***

150

Jay got up from the bed and went to the bathroom. He blotted his face with a towel and splashed a little water onto the back of his neck. Then he came back to bed. He leaned in and kissed Amber. She thought his mouth tasted funny, different. Maybe a new toothpaste. Or was it a new mouthwash? She didn't say anything, though; she kept at her sudoku, hunting for numbers.

Jay clicked off his bedside light. "I'm beat," he said. "Could barely make it through one chapter." He rolled toward her again and ran his hand along her cheekbone and down to the hollow of her neck. She gripped her pen. "I was happy to be with you today," he said. "All my friends got to see the kind of woman I ended up with. It was strange to go back and be at the school where I was a kid and confront it again—as a man."

She nodded.

Jay let out a deep breath and dropped his head into his pillow. "Night," he said.

***

Dallas tapped his foot. "Do you want to dance?" he asked.

"No," she said. "I'm most comfortable being a wallflower."

Dallas laughed, then snorted.

She thought that Dallas seemed older than Jay and didn't understand how he could've been in Jay's class. Age did funny things to people, though. He coughed a few times and sneezed into the crux of his elbow.

"Baby, Baby" played, and Amber swayed to the beat.

"I see Jay a lot," Dallas said.

"You do? When?" Amber asked.

"Well, not in person," he said. "But I see his face on bus benches whenever I'm in LA."

She laughed and pushed a strand of hair out of her eyes and took a sip of punch.

"He's a realtor, right?" he said.

"Yes."

"One time," Dallas said, slurring his words, "when my car broke down, I even sat on him for a bit. Bet he's damn good at selling houses."

"Very good, yes. Excuse me for a second."

Amber left the gym and headed to the ladies' room. The restroom was far from the gym, down a long corridor flanked with lockers. The fluorescent lights above her buzzed, and her heels made clip-clop sounds as she walked the polished asphalt. A cluster of women stood around a trashcan and smoked. Would Jay have loved her if he'd known her back then? Would they have been high school sweethearts? She was a late bloomer—sweet and kind. A lot of community service. She was seldom invited to parties, and even when she was, she rarely showed. When she and Jay met at a mutual friend's birthday long ago, she knew he was the kind of man who had always been popular. He had a way with people. He was quick with a smile, a joke, and always filled the air with conversation. He reminded her of her dear father. After working hard in law school and putting her studies ahead of men and fun, she remembered thinking that she was being rewarded with a handsome, successful man whom so many women desired.

She used the restroom and washed her hands, scrubbed them as she'd read about in a magazine, for the length of two happy birthday songs. She sung the tune a little. When she exited the ladies' room, she pulled in a deep breath and scanned the school. It was night and hard to make out the buildings, but she did her best to picture Jay, years ago, strutting the outdoor hallways, books tucked under his arm, his backpack slung over his shoulder. The school was lined with palm trees, something that was so foreign to her growing up in Seattle, and when a breeze blew, she listened to the fronds sigh.

"Whose birthday is it?" a voice said behind her. She turned.

It was Dallas.

He had a large cup in his hand, and some of his thin hair now spilled onto his forehead.

"What?" Amber said.

"You were singing 'Happy Birthday,' no?"

Amber rubbed her hands together. "Oh," she said. "We should get back in there." She began walking, her stride long and deliberate.

"When Jay gave you that ring, what'd he say?" Dallas called out. "A pearl for my pearl, or some shit like that?"

Amber stopped.

***

Soft puffs of breath worked their way from Jay's mouth. Sleep always came easy to him. The gentle light of a distant streetlamp glowed deep in the distance, and Amber gazed its way. Whenever she couldn't sleep, she always got up and looked at the streetlamp. It was silly, but she'd always found herself getting attached to things. Back in Seattle, when she was a girl, she lived on a similar looking suburban street, and often stared at a nearby lamppost that stood only a few feet from her front lawn. She often felt sorry for it: alone, in the cold, the dark, bugs hovering about its glass. One time, during the weekend, a truck pulled up. A man who worked for the city got out, pulled a ladder from the flatbed, cleaned the streetlamp's glass, and even changed the bulb inside. She smiled from her room.

Jay tugged the sheets up to his chin, and the down blanket crinkled in his grip. She returned to her sudoku but then stopped. It was enough for tonight. She clicked off her bedside light and wiggled out of her nightgown. She tossed it to the carpet, where it landed without a sound. She then yanked the soft sheets over her skin.

***

The distant pulse of music thumped at the same tempo as Amber's heart. She turned.

"A pearl for a pearl," Dallas said again. "I got it, right?" He hadn't moved at all. He was still in front of the women's restroom, leaning against a low fence.

She trudged his way and ignored the pain in her feet. When she arrived next to him, she wanted to say something but didn't know what.

"He's a conman," he said.

"Jay?"

"That's why he's good." He took a good pull of his punch and crunched on an ice cube.

A group of women walked by. One yammered on her cell phone. "It's like high school all over again," she said. "Everything's the same." The other women that were with her laughed, and they all headed into the restroom. The door shut behind them.

Amber stared at the ring, and Dallas pulled a maraschino cherry from his plastic cup, wrapped his lips around it, and ripped the fruit from the stem. "You know Jay. He's smooth. He's the man, always talking,

154

always cool. What'd he tell you he did for cash back in high school?"

She thought, then said, "He tutored. He tutored Spanish."

Dallas laughed. "*Sí, sí.*"

"Let's go back in—"

"I know it's hard to doubt that face."

Amber clasped her hands together and swallowed. The pack of women left the bathroom and cackled as they sashayed down the hall. Even though the ladies were older now, Amber could still hear the cheerleader-like quality in their voices.

***

The sheets were too heavy on her body, and Amber tossed and rolled to face her side of the room. She stared straight ahead, aligning her gaze with the distant streetlamp that burned a golden yellow. Her breath steadied, but her mind still reeled. In the early phase of their relationship, she recalled friends praising Jay's looks and warmth and generosity, even asking, "What's his catch? Is he for real?"

Night sounds reached her ears, and she was happy to hear them: another car came to a stop, and she studied the vehicle's headlights as they brushed over homes. Beside her, Jay snored. She shifted toward the edge of the bed and pressed her face into the sheets. The soft scent of laundry detergent was pleasant and familiar. She'd changed the sheets yesterday morning, before Jay had left for work. He was shaving, with lather thick on his face, when she'd come upstairs. He'd smiled at her, and his teeth seemed yellow when contrasted against the bright foam. Later, after he'd put on his tie, she fixed his collar and ran her hands over his neck.

155

"It's okay," she said to herself. It's okay, she repeated in her mind, hoping that the words would hypnotize her, but she stayed alert. All her senses sharp and focused.

***

Dallas grinned and scratched his sideburns. "That's what worked so well for him back then, when we'd go door to door in nice neighborhoods, far from here, toward La Jolla. We'd have supplies for washing carpets from my father's business. We'd say we were two high school seniors looking to make a little money for summer travel. We'd ask them if they wanted their carpets washed." Dallas sucked on his teeth. He continued: "Most people said no, but all it took was one. It was usually an older person, sometimes an older couple that was eager to talk, happy to have company. They would let us in and get us water or coffee. They'd always—"

Amber dug her nails into her palms. "How often did this happen?"

"Most Saturdays our senior year. Anyhow, we'd ask questions about who lived with them and what they were up to for the day. Most rich people—believe it or not—aren't expecting to be robbed. They're always expecting to get robbed in dirty neighborhoods, but in rich ones, they'll tell you everything. They'd let us know how long they'd lived there . . . and tell us that they were going to see a movie later in the evening. Jay would look for alarm systems and dogs, and finally, when they left us alone to do our work, we'd find a window. One that no one used. Maybe a small one in a bathroom, or behind a sofa, or a drawn curtain. We'd unlock it. We'd finish up our work, get paid thirty dollars or so, and then wait.

156

Most people get out of the house at some point on Saturday, and when they did, we were ready. We went back, found the window, and grabbed jewelry and cash—stuff that would fit in our jackets. I sold it all to pawn shops, but Jay kept a lot of the jewelry. He didn't need the money as bad as me."

Amber started to speak, then stopped.

"You should've seen how excited he was when robbing. He'd get this look—really beady eyes, and he wouldn't talk. A total pro."

**

Cold now, Amber got out of bed and slid back into her nightgown. Standing still in the bedroom, she stared at Jay's form in the sheets. Her eyes were well-acquainted with the darkness now, and she could make out his head and his left hand that lay atop the comforter. Her breath rattled, and she tried to remember some of the stories Jay had told her about the jewelry: "Bought this downtown," and "Got it at the mall," and "Found it in a boutique on Sunset . . . You know the one . . ." and "This was my mom's." She rubbed her arms, took to the bathroom, and quietly closed the door.

**

Amber's eyes snapped shut, and her face burned. She writhed in her heels and bit her bottom lip. "And this ring?"

"That was the last house we ever did, a few weeks after graduation. An older man let us in. He had this huge place. We couldn't believe that only one person lived there. We got inside and started washing carpets. He told us he was going to pick up his niece from the airport in a few hours, so he was happy the

157

carpets would be clean. I still remember the way he smelled, a little like dust. When we broke in later, I found a lot of cash in the man's office, and Jay went upstairs. Later, in the van, Jay had blood on his hands, and I asked him if he was all right. He told me that an old woman was in one of the rooms. He was going through a dresser when he found this ring and some other jewels. The woman came up behind him and startled him. He turned around and punched her. 'Just instinct, man,' I remember him saying. He said she fell back hard against a door frame. We hauled ass. Got outta there, but he didn't wash that blood off till he got back to the house. Once safe, at his home, he pulled the ring from his jacket. 'Gonna give this to a girl one day,' he said. I asked him what he was gonna tell her, and he said, 'Something stupid, like a pearl for a pearl.' We had a good laugh."

Amber didn't say a word. She stared into the distance at the dimly lit buildings. A hefty breeze blew her way and dried beads of sweat on her cheeks and nose. Even though she wasn't wearing anything other than an evening dress, she was hot. She darted to the bathroom and splashed some water on her face. Her mascara ran and dripped into the sink. She grated her face with paper towels and stood in the bathroom. When she exited, Dallas wasn't there. He was staggering down the hall. "Wait!" she yelled.

He stopped. When she reached him, she stared into his eyes. "Celebration" by Kool & the Gang danced through the air, and she had to lean in to get her words to reach Dallas's ears. "Why?" she said. And she didn't really know in which way she meant her question. Why what? she thought.

"I just thought you should know. I just thought he should return my phone calls, talk to me a little. Never hear from him anymore . . ."

158

"Maybe he wanted to change," she said.

"Oh, that look, that look in his eyes can't change," Dallas said. He headed off, not back into the gym, but down the hall, through strewn confetti, to the parking lot.

Amber clutched her chest and returned to the party. A slow song, something by Michael Bolton, she thought, played at a high volume, and the DJ, who Jay had said was the baseball coach, leaned into the microphone. "Time for a slow song," he said. "So find that special someone." She ran her eyes across the crowd, over the throng of men and women, and had trouble finding Jay but finally spotted him. His blue dress shirt was soaked with sweat. His smile was big, and he waved her over. He's thirty-eight, she thought, as she walked his way. He's lived twenty-seven years without me and eleven with me . . . I wonder which life weighs more? Jay wrapped his long arms around her and pulled her in. She clenched her jaw. "Where have you been?" he asked. "Thought I lost you." He smiled.

***

In the bathroom, Amber clicked on the light and let her eyes adjust to the brightness. Her feet were cold on the tile, so she tossed a towel to the floor and stepped onto it. She popped open the lid of her jewelry box and inspected the loot. Earrings, bracelets, watches, rings, and brooches—most of which she'd never worn— sparkled. Where exactly had they come from? She picked up a string of pearls and wrapped her fingers around each bead, savoring their smoothness and sheen. She wondered about the women who were stolen from. Were they dead? Did they have any idea who did it? Why hadn't Jay gotten rid of it all? Again, she dug her hands into the cold jewelry, felt the

159

weight, and listened to the clash of metal against metal. In time, she reached for the bathroom door and slid the lock into place.

A POODLE IN THE DESERT

My whole life, I'd only wanted two things: a Gibson Les Paul electric guitar and Pricilla Milton. Three years ago, I'd finally saved up enough money for the Gibson, but Pricilla couldn't be put on layaway. Tonight, I was going to tell her that I'd always loved her. The timing wasn't perfect; I was leaving for the Peace Corps in a couple of weeks, but I wanted her to know, and I wanted her to know it tonight, on Halloween, at my friend Scott's party.

It was a perfect Palm Springs night: seventy-nine degrees, dry, with the sky as open as the freeway. The rush of air buffeted my face as I sped up and leaned my Vespa into a bend. In less than five minutes, I was at Scott's. I hopped off my scooter and secured my helmet to the handlebar. Masses of children rushed the sidewalks in all directions, and parents stood tall in the centers of these clusters, holding flashlights and calling out names and "Be careful," and "Slow down," and "Watch out," and "Joey, your cape fell off," and "It's back there," and "Yes, on your left . . . your other left, on Mrs. Brody's hedge."

At that age, all I wanted to do was be an adult, shave like Dad, and wear dress shirts, but now, at twenty-four, I missed the freedom of being a boy, of having no other goal for the entire month of October than to possess more candy than the other kids in the neighborhood. I just wanted to tell those children buzzing around the street, with their superhero tights tucked into their sneakers, that adulthood was nothing more than candy corn: it looked exciting, but it was really sticky and turned stale fast.

Music, laughter, and loud conversation hung in the air around Scott's house. I twisted the knob and entered. "Hey, Cooper," Scott said. He was dressed as an old-fashioned donut. He also had a backward cap on, which I wasn't sure what to do with—was he a rebellious sweet treat? One that just didn't want to jump into the fryer? "When do you head off to Ghana again?" he asked, leading me into a hallway where Led Zeppelin's "Black Dog" had trouble finding us.

"Where's Pricilla?"

"Man, I'm gonna miss you. Can't you just do some hero shit out here in Palm Springs? The freeway's full of trash. What the hell are you, anyway? Hipster Santa?"

"What? No. I'm Mister Rogers."

"Oh, yeah. I see it. The red cardigan, the sneakers. You're the casual Mister Rogers, the 'just in the house' guy. How'd you get your hair gray?"

"Baby powder. Is Pricilla here?"

"Been here a while. By the firepit in the backyard, I think. She asked when you were coming a few times." Scott patted me on the shoulder and started mingling with a woman dressed as a slutty construction worker. A long blond braid poked out from underneath her hard hat.

I walked outside, where my eyes found Pricilla. They always did. I took a deep breath, then another, and tried to get my heart to relax, but it couldn't. She was no longer in front of the firepit; she was near the edge of Scott's property, sitting on a bench in a garden that Scott had let go to hell. I strolled her way, reminding myself to breathe slowly so that my face wouldn't match my sweater. "Hey, Pricilla," I said.

She turned my way and uncrossed her legs. She was dressed as Dorothy from *The Wizard of Oz*, and she had it all, too: the blue-and-white-checkered dress

163

with two big shoulder straps secured by white buttons, a ruffled blouse underneath, a wicker basket in her hand, and ankle-high socks tucked into shiny ruby-red slippers. "Hi, Coop," she said.

"You all right?" Even with the poor outdoor lighting, I noticed that her eyes were shiny and that her cheeks were wet.

"I lost Roberto."

"Your little poodle?"

"Yes. I brought him with me, you know, to look like Toto."

I joined her on the bench. "Why are we here, then? Have you looked for him?"

"Of course! I'm just tired now. I thought maybe he never left the party or that someone was playing with him or something."

"Let's go find him! He can't be that far. His legs are the size of golf pencils."

"Okay," she said, grabbing hold of my hand. We headed across the burnt grass, through the house, and out the front door. Her fingers and palm were soft and delicate, and I wanted to hold them tighter but worried that I'd crush her. I hadn't seen her cry since her father's funeral some years ago. Poor Mr. Milton had suffered a heart attack. And before that, I think she'd let out a few tears when Hal McGinnis broke up with her in the eleventh grade. She'd rambled on and on about how sweet guys were an endangered species, and I'd just sat there in the cafeteria, poking at my sloppy joe.

When would I tell her? It couldn't be now. She was frantic and worried. I'd wait.

Once we reached the driveway, I called out, "Roberto! Roberto!"

Nothing.

Then Pricilla did the same: "Roberto! Roberto!"

A chunky kid, not far down the block, who I thought was dressed as the Flash, yelled back, "Yeah, what do you need?"

Pricilla sighed. I apologized to the Flash and told him we were looking for another Roberto.

"I love him," Pricilla said, "but he's a stupid dog." She paused and looked me up and down. "Who are you supposed to be? Norman Rockwell?"

"I'm Mister Rogers."

"The cowboy? No, wait, that's Roy Rogers. I love Mister Rogers, the 'hello, neighbor' guy, right? He was so sweet."

"Yeah—"

"Wait!" Pricilla pointed to a house in the distance. "I think I see him. Right there! I just saw a little white dot. It has to be him! Roberto!"

I chased Pricilla who chased Roberto who chased freedom. We ran against the grain of trick-or-treaters, weaving through capes and hats and brooms and axes. Pricilla had decided to name her dog Roberto after the ballplayer Roberto Clemente, her dad's favorite player. Mr. Milton I had always thought secretly rooted for me to date his daughter. He'd always hugged me whenever I came through the door and told me I looked "sharp." I'd been with Pricilla when she got news of her father. We were at my apartment, playing Scrabble. I had just plunked down *quibble* and couldn't have been more excited. She started crying in a way I'd never seen, her whole body convulsing, and her face turning white. I scooted over on the couch and held her. I wanted someone to cry like that over me. I wanted to mean that much to someone.

"Did you see that?" Pricilla said. "Did you see him?"

We approached a dark house that was clearly not interested in Halloween: the lights were off, the shades were closed, and the sprinklers misted the front lawn. We dashed across the wet grass to a side gate where Pricilla said she definitely saw Roberto. She crouched and peeked through the planks of wood. She yanked the gate open, and the hinges groaned like my Uncle Bart getting out of a waterbed.

"Roberto," she whispered as we tiptoed past trashcans and an open barbecue.

I delivered the famous line about not being in Kansas and then regretted it.

"I wondered how long it would take you to say that. There!" She hurried into the backyard. "Berto! Berto!"

An automatic light cut on, casting a thick cone of white across the backyard, temporarily stunning us. I thought I heard a rustle at the far end of the lawn, but by the time Pricilla got there, Berto was gone. She called his name a few more times, but nothing. I wrapped my arms around her. She smelled like coconut. I knew I'd never find another woman like her, not in Russia, not in Ghana, not even in America. There was only one. So many men searched for a Pricilla, and I was lucky to have grown up with one. We'd lost teeth, time, and Toto together.

All of my happiest moments took place in her presence, and I knew it'd be strange to spend years away from her. She'd told me she'd visit and that she was proud of me, but I knew I'd return home soon and she'd be with some bastard named Brad or Hoyt or Zach, a man with meaty shoulders and thick ringlets of golden hair. Some dude with a tough-guy job, like a firefighter or a lion tamer. He'd have an old Corvette or Buick that he'd polish on weekends with a special microfiber towel, and Pricilla would make her famous mango lemonade and bring it out to him while he worked on the transmission. Meanwhile, across town, I'd be married to Barbara, a mailwoman, whose father, Don, hated my charity-giving vegetarian guts and who often said at get-togethers, "Real men eat bacon!"

"We'll get him," I said. "We'll find him."

She brought her hand up and clutched mine.

A sliding door on the back porch screeched open. The automatic light clicked on again and backlit a man with the physique of a Russian doll. The man held a rake. "What the hell are you two doing in my yard?" he said in a voice that was more Kentucky than California.

Pricilla walked the man's way. "I'm sorry, sir. I've lost my dog. He's a curly white little poodle. I saw him make his way in here. I wasn't thinking. I'm sorry."

"Lucky I didn't shoot you both."

"With a rake?" I said, joining Pricilla near the deck stairs.

"Who the hell are you supposed to be?" the man asked. "Ronald Reagan?"

"He's Mister Rogers," Pricilla said.

"Never liked that cupcake," the man said.

"Cupcake?" I said.

A woman's voice escaped from inside the dark home. "Harold?" the voice said. "What is it? Is it a prowler?"

The man turned around and faced the sliding door. "Shut up, Marjorie. Go back to bed."

Pricilla raised her eyebrows.

"Don't talk to her like that," I said.

"Thank you," said Marjorie.

"Mind your business, kid," the man said. He pointed the rake's teeth at me and trudged my way. Pricilla wedged her body next to mine. The coconut scent lingered in the air and gave me confidence. "She was just asking what happened. Marjorie," I shouted, "we were just searching for a dog. We thought—"

The man stomped onto the grass and brought the rake back. Marjorie yelled, "Thank you," and Harold told her to close the door and pipe down, and I told him to be quiet and calm himself, and then he came at us faster. For a big guy, he could really move. In the distance, I thought I heard a dog bark, but I wasn't sure until Pricilla confirmed it. "It's Berto Boy!" she said.

"Run!" I said. "Run!"

We zipped down the side of the house. Harold followed. I even felt a gust of wind as he swung the rake and it nearly connected with my back. Instead, though, it slammed a bag of charcoal next to the barbecue. "Always hated Reagan," he said before Pricilla kicked open the gate, and we sped to the other side of the street and slipped into an alley.

From there, we studied Harold in his driveway, his head craning from side to side, the rake in his hands. A few children bustled past and pointed at the old man. One of them giggled and asked, "Who is he, Mama? Elmer Fudd?"

When things were calmer, Pricilla and I left the alley, took to the street, and resumed the search. I scoured the sidewalks and front lawns of homes, creepily whispering, "Roberto" and "Berto Boy," and Pricilla asked oncoming trick-or-treaters if they'd seen a curly little white dog. One of the girls whom she'd asked wasn't any taller than a fire hydrant and was dressed as a pumpkin.

In this moment, I was perfectly happy. From time to time, life seemed soft and mellow, as if I were roaming an unshaken snow globe. This warming feeling didn't happen to me a lot, but when it did, the common denominator seemed to be Pricilla. I remembered when I'd first gotten my driver's license and my dad gave me his LeBaron for the night and we put the top down and didn't have a destination. I drove and drove, and Pricilla controlled the music, and we rushed past speed-limit signs and thanked them for the suggestion. That was all I wanted now: just the two of us—and maybe Roberto—on my Vespa, cutting through the desert night.

I neared Pricilla and the pumpkin. The girl told Pricilla that she thought she'd seen a dog in the haunted house up the road, and Pricilla leaned forward and placed her hands on her thighs.

"So right up the road?" I asked the girl. "You think you saw him?"

"I saw a little dog," the girl said, "just right up there. Who are you supposed to be?"

"Mister Rogers."

"You look like my dad."

The girl's what-must-have-been chaperone called her name, Joy, and the girl skipped away. I'd never seen a pumpkin skip.

"Do you know what's wrong with kids today?" I asked Pricilla as we started the climb toward the haunted house.

"Oh, please, not another one of your rants."

"No Mister Rogers. He died, and all kids became weird."

Pricilla shook her head.

In those soft moments between conversation, when I could hear telephone wires buzz and light gusts dance overhead, I started to ask Pricilla. Actually, I just said, "You know what?" and "How long have we known each other?" Then I calmed down. I knew she'd say, "We're like brother and sister," and that the whole thing would be over. Asking a long-time friend to be more than that was like leaping across a lava-filled moat: most people never survived the jump.

"You know," she said, "the only people happier than children on Halloween must be dentists. I bet right now, they're just sitting in their living rooms, sharpening their tools, thinking of what kinds of cars to buy."

"Dentists don't sharpen tools," I said.

"It was for effect," she said.

I smiled. And she started jogging. Soon after I'd broken a sweat, we arrived at the haunted house. It was built of plywood and began on the driveway and led into the garage. A woman dressed as a witch with a wart above her top lip spread both of her hands out, as if to say, "Welcome."

"Ma'am," Pricilla said, "have you seen a little dog? He goes by Roberto."

She didn't answer. Witches didn't help people, apparently.

"Lady," I said, "can you drop character for just a moment? We've lost our dog. He looks like a large rat."

"Cooper!" Pricilla said.

"I'm trying to put it in terms she might understand."

The woman stood there, continuing to motion the way of the entrance. Her wart seemed to have gotten bigger in the last minute. Maybe I should have asked *it* for help. Pricilla shrugged, and we headed inside the haunted house. When I turned back around, the witch was taking a sip of orange soda. Good sorceresses didn't speak, but Fanta was okay.

Inside, it was the expected mess: strobing lights, fake spiders, cobwebs, eerie *whoo-wee-woo* music, and a labyrinth-like layout. Corridor after corridor was splashed with fake blood (I hoped) and strewn with little plastic bones and cut-up Barbie dolls.

"Roberto!" Pricilla said. "Roberto!"

A machine hissed, and a cloud of gray smoke blanketed us. "Why does this fake fog always smell like feet? It's not scary. It's just gross," I said. "And why the hell would Roberto come in here? He looks smart . . . you know? Those big eyes, they look intelligent. I really hope we don't die this way, in here, like this. Can you imagine dying in here, this way, wrapped in this smelly fog?"

"Shut up, Coop," Pricilla said. She reached out, and our fingers met somewhere in the smoke. I held her tight as the music swelled and the *Psycho* theme pulsed. She screamed, and I clutched her shoulder.

We crept forward. Baby steps. Our feet sliding along the garage floor. A group of people in front of us squealed, and the lights shut off. Then a red glow took hold of the tight passage.

"My earring! I lost my earring!" Pricilla dropped to her knees and began sliding her hands over the ground.

"Can you do me a huge favor and stop losing stuff?"

"Seriously, Coop. Help me. I actually felt it fall out, so it's got to be right around here."

Red light morphed into blue light and blue light into pale light. We were both on the ground now, on all fours, massaging the garage floor. I had never told a girl I loved her. Sure, I'd used *love* to describe everything from *The Great Gatsby* to couscous, but I found it sad that I'd never used the word the way it wanted to be used. And while I knew I was far from an expert in the matter of love, I was certain that love was being spread out on a garage floor, searching for an earring while searching for Roberto.

"I didn't know Dorothy wore earrings," I said.

"She didn't," Pricilla shouted. "There's just more pressure on girls these days."

"Oh, I think I found it," I said. "No, no, that's just gum—still *very* wet gum."

Pricilla called off the hunt soon after. "I liked those earrings. Bought 'em just for tonight."

"You still have one, though, right?"

"Yeah."

"You can just wear the one, then—like Michael Jordan."

"That's who I try to look like."

I helped her up, and we pressed on through the dark, stinky maze. Again, the fog blasted us, and I gripped Pricilla. Moments like these, when Pricilla was mine and no one else's, were my favorite. I savored them. Replayed them. Did my best to pump them with formaldehyde.

It did annoy me that while in my arms, she constantly called out another name, Roberto, but I reminded myself that he was, in fact, a poodle, and not an Antonio Banderas look-alike with curly chest hair and a soothing Spanish accent that would turn *Pricilla* into *Pree-cee-la*.

One step at a time, we conquered the haunted house.

"Do you *see* it?"

"What?"

"That." She pointed at a black mass, fifteen feet in the distance. "It's coming at us!"

"It's not Roberto," I said.

"No," she said, "it's not Roberto."

We worked north. The thing plodded south. We crept. The thing lumbered. Pricilla squeezed my hand, and I squeezed back.

"If need be, I'll kick its ass," I said.

"Sure," Pricilla said.

I could hear the thing breathe.

In and out.

Hard and quick.

Then it laughed and let a high-pitched scream rip from its throat. The noise assailed my ears, and I dropped Pricilla's hand and shielded my head. She shrieked and swung her wicker basket and smacked me in the neck. I may have called out for help, too. I think I even yelled, "Heavens to Betsy" a few times.

"Ow!" Pricilla said. "You shit! You bit me!"

"Let go of me, lady!" a voice said, a squeaky voice.

"What the hell is going on?" I asked.

Pricilla stormed toward the opening, all the while holding on to whatever had bitten her. The voice spouted bits of apologies, and I followed the two of them until we reached the driveway. The witch had vanished, and the chomping monster turned out to be a little boy wearing a Batman costume. It wasn't even one of those cool Batman costumes, either—the ones with built-in six-pack abs and hearty pecs. No, this one's bat emblem was fuzzy, like shag carpeting, and some of the spandex, especially in the belly area, looked tired and see-through. Even the mask wasn't right, with droopy, dachshund-like ears.

"I'm sorry," Baby Batman said.

"What kind of an asshole bites someone?" I said.

"Coop, don't swear at him," said Pricilla. "Seriously, though, why did you bite me?" She showed him her hand. There was a red semicircle where her index finger and thumb met.

"I just got excited," Baby Batman said. "You both screamed, and then I felt I had to do something scary, but I didn't know what."

173

"I don't think you understand the Batman thing," I said. "You're supposed to be on *our* side. You should be *fighting* the monsters. Batman would never scare people."

"I didn't want to be Batman," the boy said. "My mom just got me this because it was on sale."

"Batman on sale?" Pricilla said.

"Walmart," Baby Batman said.

"Honor the costume," I said. "Look. She's Dorothy. She's honoring the costume. You don't see her holding up a liquor store. Do you?"

He nodded and hung his head.

"It's okay," Pricilla said, shooting me a look that said, "Take it easy."

"It's all right, Baby Batman," I said, patting him on the back. "More importantly, have you seen a dog? A curly white little dog. He goes by the name Roberto."

"There was a dog here earlier, but he was grayish and kind of big."

"Oh," Pricilla said. "Really?" She put her head in her hands, and Baby Batman patted her on the back. I did, too.

In time, I wrapped one of my arms around Pricilla and guided her away from the haunted house. We took to the road, our shoes scraping along the yellow-lit asphalt. What would happen if I found the dog? Would Pricilla need me to stay? Would she want me to stay? Or would she just thank me and move on? I worked up some courage and said, "I just don't understand it. Why would anyone want to run away from you?"

"You are."

"I'm not running. I'm right here."

"You're leaving, though."

174

"I've never been closer to anyone, Pricilla . . ." And then I couldn't speak. My mouth turned into cracked desert clay. Romance with Pricilla was a language I couldn't speak.

She waited a while, called out for Roberto a few times, then said, "I'll come visit."

"I really hope you do."

"By the way, thanks for letting go of my hand when we got attacked by Baby Batman. Did you really yell, 'Heavens to Betsy,' too? The cardigan has seeped into your pores."

"I didn't let go."

"You *so* did. Then you screamed *way* louder than me and dropped me like a sack of potatoes."

"Never understood that expression. Who the hell is dropping all of these potatoes? And why? Spuds are fragile."

"The one that always gets me is blowing smoke up your ass."

"Yeah, the visual's strange, too, right? And is it cigarette smoke? Hookah? What kind of smoke are we talking about?"

"Roberto!" she let out a few times. She peeked under a parked car. I called out for him. Then we both yelled his name. "Are you sad about leaving?" She blinked her eyes, and the streetlights' sheen caught the hazel of her irises.

"Yeah. I know I'll be doing good stuff, though, so that helps." I couldn't believe I'd just described the honorable JFK-founded institution known as the Peace Corps with the words *doing good stuff*.

"Roberto!" Pricilla said.

"I want you to know that you're my favorite person in the world," I said.

Pricilla stared at the ground and dug one of her shoes into the asphalt, working it back and forth. "I'm

175

going to miss you, too," she said. Then she broke the quiet with another "Roberto!"

"Do you remember that night? The night when we drove around town in my dad's LeBaron? Do you?" I said.

"With no place to go," she said.

"Yeah." I noticed the glimmer of her single earring and nearly laughed.

"I wish we could do that again," she said. "It's hard to spend a lot of time together these days. I'm busy with my master's and work, and you're trying to save the world."

"I liked when our only thing was hanging out. Like spending time with you was a day of the week, you know?"

"Then we went to different colleges," she said.

"Yeah, but we stayed close, right?" I said. "We talked on the phone a lot, and we both moved back home right after graduation."

"Now you're abandoning me again," she said. As I thought of a reply, a police car grumbled up the street. Its roof lights spun and flashed, but the sirens weren't on. "I'm going to ask about Roberto," Pricilla said. She waved her arms, and the police car pulled alongside her. The officer lowered his window and clicked on the interior light. He was around thirty, with a perfectly shaven face. How was he *so* well shaven? Had he *just* started his shift? Did he use a straight razor? Maybe he had one of those shower mirrors that allowed you to shave while warm in a blanket of steam. Pricilla leaned against the driver's-side door. Why did she need to get so close? He could hear her just fine.

"How can I help you, Dorothy?" the officer said. He smiled. Of course, his teeth were all in a row.

176

"Who are you supposed to be?" He looked my way. "A grandpa?"

I just went with it. "Yes, a big ol' grandpa."

He smiled.

"My dog," Pricilla said. She told him the story.

The officer picked up his radio and asked a question about a curly white little dog. The man actually got to say "over" and "copy that" for a living. Pricilla seemed impressed. She kept smoothing out her left braid. After he radioed in the message, we waited, and Pricilla filled in the empty moments. "Busy night?" she asked.

"Yeah," the officer said.

"You probably have a lot of wild stories."

"For sure. I just arrested a man who was dressed as Jesus. He was disturbing the peace in a mini-mart. You from around here, Dorothy?"

Pricilla giggled. "Yes. Born and raised. You?"

I knew he was falling for Pricilla. It was easy to do—everyone had, did, and would.

"I just moved out here, was transferred from Barstow. I really like it. There's enough action, but not too much, you know?"

"Do you ever get scared?" Pricilla said.

"He's human, Pricilla," I said. "Of course he—"

"There's no time for fear," he said.

No time for fear? What did that even mean? "Roberto! Roberto! Pricilla, we should get back to looking for Roberto."

The two of them played verbal Ping-Pong. He asked about what she did for a living, and she let him know that she was working toward a special education degree and waitressing in the meantime. He told her how much he respected teachers and how they should get paid more and that they were unsung heroes, and

177

Pricilla laughed and leaned back and said, "Me? A hero? I'm just a girl—a little desert girl."

A little desert girl? What the shit?

The police station finally radioed back, answering my prayer and telling Officer Fearless that no one had reported a curly white little dog but that they had found a beagle wandering down Main Street.

"Sorry about that," the officer said. "Let me get your information. I'll let you know if we find a little white dog."

Police officers were lucky. They could ask a woman for her "information," not her number. "Information" didn't seem as threatening, yet it was the very same stuff. While Pricilla took her time giving him her number, I stepped off to a nearby driveway, pulled out my phone, and dialed the number for the local police. I had it saved on my phone from the time my Vespa had been stolen. When the secretary picked up, I told her what I saw: "Yes," I said, thinking of an address that was close enough to get Officer Flirty dispatched. "I have something to report." The woman on the other end of the line asked me to go ahead. "I'm in the Walmart parking lot, and there's this man harassing this beautiful lady. She's trying to get away, but he won't leave her alone. He's being an asshole and pestering her, and I can't get him to stop. Can you send someone out here?" The woman said she was on it, and I hung up, shoved my phone deep into my cardigan pocket, and returned to Pricilla and the officer. The sweet sound of grainy CB radio popped into the night air: "Attention units: We have a possible 8-0-8 in the Walmart parking lot. Nearby units . . ."

Pricilla howled with laughter at one of the officer's jokes.

"Shouldn't you . . . Sounds like you should get that. It's real close. A possible 808," I said.

178

"Yes," Pricilla agreed. "They need you. You're important."

"Yeah, guess so," the officer said. He put his car in gear and flipped on more lights, but not before reaching toward Pricilla and saying, "We'll be in touch." He sped off, the sound of his American engine booming.

"He told me that the pound closed hours ago, so there's no point in looking there," Pricilla said.

"Sorry," I said. "A lot of the time, a dog goes back to where he's most comfortable or even the spot where he first got lost."

"This isn't like him. He usually doesn't like to spend any time away from me."

"I hear ya."

We started back toward the house, calling out for Roberto every now and then. The street had changed its costume, too: it was no longer teeming with children and parents and candy and laughter. I thought of those kids shoving their favorite costumes back into dresser drawers for the long year. What use was it to tell Pricilla how I felt about her? I was leaving. She didn't need me to come clean. It was selfish, actually. "Hi, I've always loved you. Bye." It was better to be a weakling and her friend than a hero and her nothing.

Scott's party was still going strong. Laughter and banter exploded from the home like fireworks, and I leaned against my Vespa and tried to look cool while Pricilla sat on the curb and fanned her dress over her knees. "I really love him. It's silly maybe to love something so much, something that's incapable of loving you back. Here I am, searching and looking everywhere."

I joined her on the curb. "He does love you back. He's your Berto Boy."

179

There was a yip.

A bark.

And then another.

They were muffled and seemingly nearby. "In the house, I think," Pricilla said. "Go check the house! I'll stay here, just in case. Hurry! Go!"

I sped off, my laced-up sneakers bashing the pavement, and shoved Scott's front door open and hurried about the floor plan. I scoured the living room, the bedrooms, the backyard, the kitchen, the garage, and a bathroom (which a man dressed as Zorro had forgotten to lock). I was certain I'd heard a bark.

Had I heard Pricilla correctly? "Maybe it's silly to love something so much, something that's incapable of loving you back." Roberto was a dumbass who licked his crotch for fun. He didn't realize how lucky he was to get caressed by Pricilla's hands and bathed in her porcelain tub and granted permission to sleep at the foot of her bed. He was the luckiest son of a bitch on the planet.

"The dog!" I said to Scott. I wiped my forehead with the sleeve of my sweater. "Have you seen Pricilla's dog?"

"No." He tilted back a beer.

"Shit."

"Did you check upstairs? When did she lose her dog?"

I pushed through a crowd of costumed folks and rushed up the stairs, yanking on the railing, flying up to the second story. There, I got on all fours, thinking I'd have a better chance of spotting Berto if I got on his level. "Roberto! Berto! Berto Boy!"

Behind each door was exactly what was supposed to be, though: beds in bedrooms, books in bookcases, baths in bathrooms. I really thought I'd find him and that I'd be Pricilla's cardigan-wearing hero.

But nothing. I got off the ground and shuffled into a bathroom. I pulled in a few breaths, splashed some water on my face, then gazed out the tiny window on to the street. Pricilla brought her head back and forth, and her pigtails swayed. After checking the surroundings, she slinked to her car and plucked what had to be keys from her wicker basket. She slowly opened the driver's-side door and scanned the road once again. Inside her car, sitting on the seat, was Roberto—the curly little white dog. He was wagging his tail, barking, and licking Pricilla.

Heat rushed to my cheeks, and my chest tingled. I balled my fists to keep my fingers from twitching and held Pricilla in sight. She placed Roberto in her basket and shut her car door with a quick thud, before taking a few more steps into the center of the road and casting her gaze about the quiet street. There was something perfect about Pricilla Milton standing in the middle of Yucca Lane, alone, waiting to tell me that she'd found Roberto, that he'd just turned up. I didn't know why she'd done it. Maybe she'd wanted the same thing all along, or maybe she'd thought an adventure would pull it out of me, or maybe we'd just needed to search for something that was never lost in the first place.

And so, I sprinted from the bathroom, jumping the stairs by twos, with the front door in sight and the knowledge that Pricilla and Roberto were standing behind it.

THE TRAIN'S DISTANT WHISTLE

Tiffany scrawled her name, smoothed the single sheet of paper with her hands, and brought the letter to the couch, combing over the sentences for mistakes. She didn't know what she'd do if she were to find an error—rewrite the whole thing?—but it was habit. There were a couple of spots where she thought she needed commas, and she was able to squeeze in the little curves. One more time, she read the last paragraph: "I know what I saw, Art. I know what I feel. I just wish you'd been honest. Were you confused or just chickenshit?" She ran her tongue over her teeth and placed the letter under a tissue box on the coffee table.

So far, the Santa Barbara summer days had been perfection. The heat was alive in the daytime, but now, at six in the evening, the air cooled and gained moisture. As a breeze pushed through a screened window and fell upon Tiffany's face, a knock at her front door punctuated the silence.

Her heart jolted, and her neck stiffened. The last time anyone had come inside her home was months ago, when a handyman had entered to fix the garbage disposal. She didn't like people, preferring to stay tucked away in her home where she was distant from society's judgments and stares. "Hello?" A voice that she couldn't make out warbled through the door.

Excuses for a potential Jehovah's Witness or solicitor started unfurling: an appointment, sickness, picking someone up at the airport. Then, she thought she heard a little girl's voice penetrate the hardwood door. "She's so . . ."

She's so *what?* Weird? Lonely? Obese? It was nothing she hadn't heard before. She fanned her hair off her shoulders and yanked the door open.

Three people stood on the welcome mat. They were Tiffany's down-the-road neighbors, a young family, who had only moved in a few months ago.

"Tiffany, right?" the man said. He wore smudged glasses and had nice straight teeth. He was flanked by a waifish woman and a little girl who couldn't have been more than nine. The girl's eyes were watery. "We're the Gibbons family, the new neighbors. We met the other day when a package accidentally—"

"I remember," Tiffany said, wanting to add, "Why are you here?"

"Anyway . . . so sorry to do this to you, but could you watch Kayla for a little bit? My brother was in a car accident, and my wife and I have to go to the hospital. We can't reach the sitter, and we can't leave her alone."

"The hospital is no place for her," the woman said. "Would you mind?"

"Please," the man said.

Tiffany looked down, spotting the girl's saddle shoes that were stained brown at the toes. "That would be fine," she said. "I'm sorry to hear about your brother."

"Thank you," the man said. "I'm Ben, by the way."

"Leslie," the woman said.

"And that's Kayla," the man added.

Tiffany nodded, telling herself that she could place the letter in an envelope and address it later. The mail had long since passed anyhow.

"Go ahead," the man said to his daughter. "It'll be okay. Tiffany's very kind."

Kayla blinked and entered Tiffany's home.

"Thanks again, Tiffany," the woman said. She and the man scurried to the road, where their SUV idled.

Once the door was shut, Kayla peered at the floor in the foyer and twisted in place, her black curly hair lifting with each swoop.

Tiffany led Kayla to the couch, thinking about how the evening had changed from open-endedness to responsibility. "How old are you?" Tiffany asked. Kayla held up her hands, showing four fingers on one and three on the other. Then she muttered something softly. "What was that?" Tiffany asked.

Kayla brought her knees up and placed her shoes on the couch. "My uncle is going to die."

Tiffany stood and turned off the ceiling fan so she could better hear the girl. "You don't know that," she said.

Kayla's eyes aligned with Tiffany's stomach and stayed there. "I saw my dad cry."

"You did?"

"He never cries."

"It was a really bad accident?"

"I think so." The girl nodded. "Have a lot of people in your family died?"

"Yes."

"Is it sad?"

"Sometimes, it's sadder when people you love are still around, 'cause you know they could be better."

Kayla wiped her eyes with the heel of her hand and asked Tiffany whether she had a tissue. Tiffany pointed to the box on the coffee table, then went into the kitchen and returned with two glasses filled with ice and grape juice. They drank, and Tiffany turned on the television. *After Dusk* was on, an apocalyptic film that Tiffany had seen in bits here and there but never

185

in its entirety. The end of time never frightened her, though. Our current existence—the one where we had to live with our choices—seemed far more terrifying than a world rife with fireballs and ice chunks. The movie, however, did seem to console Kayla. She propped her saddle shoes up on the coffee table near her glass of juice, folded her arms, and studied the screaming people and mythical waves. "Is it just you in this house?" Kayla asked during a commercial.

Tiffany muted the volume. "Yes."

"Do you have a husband?"

"Not anymore," Tiffany said.

"How about a cat or hamster?"

"No. I don't want to take care of anything."

Kayla squirmed on the couch, trying to pull her dress out from underneath her body. In her attempt, she kicked out her legs and toppled her glass of grape juice. The purple liquid and crescent moons of ice flooded the coffee table, saturating the letter that Tiffany had spent hours writing. Once she spotted the paper, heavy with liquid, she shut her eyes and stopped. She sank her teeth into her cheek and heard droplets splatter from the table onto the hardwood floor. Her heart sped, and a twinge radiated in her lower back. Sure, she could write the letter again, but would she want to?

"Oops," Kayla said.

Tiffany stood and stared at the mess. The coffee table was constructed of white tiles, which would wipe clean, but the liquid had managed to funnel into the gray grout and disperse through the straight lines. She studied the juice as it pushed forward and then turned her attention to the sopping letter. Could she even find those words again? Could a volcano ever erupt the same way twice? "*Oops.* That's all you have to say?" Tiffany tried to keep her voice steady but felt her words gaining momentum. "I was fine. You think I don't have anything better to do than watch you?" Kayla clutched a nearby cushion and placed it atop her lap. "That's what everyone says, 'Oh, I bet that fat woman down the street isn't busy. I bet she wouldn't mind helping us out.'" Tiffany stopped. Kayla's eyes grew glassy, and she hopped up and walked to the coffee table, plucking pieces of glass off the floor. "Jesus! Don't touch that!" Tiffany said, unaware that the glass had apparently tumbled off the side of the table and broken into several jagged pieces. She hurried to the kitchen, where she flung open the cabinet doors and grabbed some paper towels, a sponge, and a bucket.

In time, Tiffany started cleaning the table, wadding up paper towels, and absorbing the juice. Even though Tiffany had told her not to, Kayla continued picking up glass. "Who's Art?" Kayla said, staring at the note.

Tiffany snatched the letter from her and tossed it into the bucket, where the wet paper landed with a thunk. Soon, the table was clean. The grout where the juice had rested was darker, but in time, the color might lighten. Kayla picked up the last jagged bit of glass and dropped it into the bucket, this time cutting herself. Her blood was practically the same color as the juice, and Tiffany rushed to the kitchen, setting the cleaning supplies on the floor and grabbing a Band-Aid. "I'm sorry," Kayla called to her.

Tiffany made sure the wound was clean before adhering the Band-Aid. "It doesn't do much good to talk about it," Tiffany said.

Kayla nodded, thanked Tiffany for the Band-Aid, and took a seat in the recliner across from the couch where Tiffany was seated.

Through the open windows, Tiffany could hear the train sound its whistle as it zoomed alongside Highway 101. The train was consistent, and it always amazed her how a horn that loud could sometimes be ignored and sink into the ambient sounds of life; then, at other times, it was startling how hard the whistle blew, seemingly tearing apart the quiet.

"Was the letter hard to write?" Kayla said.

Tiffany stared at a moth that fluttered against a screen's tight wires searching for any possible way in and combing over the metal again and again. "It was. Yes."

"Was Art your husband?" Kayla asked. Tiffany felt as if she was back in the wood-paneled medical building where she'd sought treatment for her depression. "Did you love him?"

Tiffany didn't want to answer these questions but figured it was the best way for Kayla to forget about the recent coffee-table outburst. "Of course."

"I love my uncle," Kayla said.

"When I was your age, I remember begging each night for God to let my friends, family, and dogs live to be a million."

"You did?"

"Yeah. Now I'm old enough to know that love of any sort is just delayed pain."

The apocalypse movie showed the ocean growing in mass, swirling, and beginning to swallow the Statue of Liberty.

"Where is he now?"

"Not here, right?" Tiffany fluffed a cushion, recalling that Saturday last year, the thirteenth of December. Art had just gotten out of the shower, his body rosy; Tiffany was reading a spy novel. He'd started with a cliché: "I need to talk to you." And had ended with something new: "I'm gay."

"Is he dead?"

"In a way, I suppose he is."

"Then why did you write him a letter?"

Tiffany stood and turned the ceiling fan back on. She leaned against the window where the moth continued to buzz and flicked at the insect. "We're divorced."

"I hope the doctors save my uncle. He always wears these ties with cartoon characters on them and brings me sour candy when he comes over." Kayla continued to yammer, and Tiffany wondered about Art. More than anything, the letter served as a way of letting him know that she was still alive. When Tiffany tuned back into the conversation, Kayla was still gibbering about her uncle and the special oven he had in his backyard for making pizzas. What impressed Tiffany about love was that it wasn't learned. It was innate. No one ever taught someone to love; rather, the ability was developed from an early age, like language, but instead of vowels and consonants, it was passed through waves and gazes. "Is he married to someone else now?" Kayla said.

Tiffany sat back down on the couch. "I think so."

"My friend's mom and dad just got divorced. I hope my mom and dad don't do that. Sometimes they scream."

The bark of a neighbor's dog cut through the air. "Screaming isn't leaving, though."

"That's Tommy's dog."

"What?"

"My neighbor. He has a big dog that barks *only* at night."

Tiffany grinned. "I hear him now and then."

"Why did he leave?"

Tiffany crossed her legs. "What's your favorite toy right now?"

"I have a lot."

"But your *favorite* one . . ."

"I like my doll, Tweenie."

"Do you think you'll love Tweenie forever?"

"Yes," she said, picking at her Band-Aid.

"That's good." Tiffany thought that if she hadn't put on so much weight after her father's death that maybe Art would have stayed attracted to her. When she'd married him seven years ago, she was a little heavy, but after the loss of her dad, she'd turned to sweets to curb her sadness, while Art stayed in impeccable shape. The last time she'd weighed herself, two months ago, she was 311 pounds. These days, she was so disgusted with her image that she'd done away with all the mirrors in her home—something that no one noticed because she never had anyone over. When she traveled for business, which was rare, her first objective was to pin towels over the mirrors. There were times, though, when she accidentally caught a glimpse of herself in store windows or in restaurant bathrooms, and it made her want to do nothing other than eat.

"If my uncle dies, how long will I be sad?"

"Who knows?" Tiffany said. "The sadness never really goes away. You just get used to it being there."

"Really?"

"In a way, the heartache is all you have, so you don't want it to totally leave."

"Like a year?" Kayla asked, retying one of her shoes.

"Everyone's got their own speed, I guess." Whenever she replayed visions of Art, the same images came to mind: the way he shaved his head every other day, how he always turned his socks right side out before dropping them into the hamper, and his weird routine of always kissing Tiffany on the bridge of her nose before bedtime.

Once Kayla's shoelace was tied, she got up from the recliner and took a seat on the couch next to Tiffany. They watched the end of the movie with the sound still muted. Throngs of people evacuated buildings, and the Hollywood sign lost many of its letters until it just spelled HOLY. When Tiffany looked to her right, she noticed Kayla's head, flush against her arm. She'd never felt the contact, not even the slightest sensation. "I wish I could tell my uncle how much I love him, but I know he wouldn't be able to hear me."

"In your mind, you can tell him whatever you want as many times as you want," Tiffany said. She'd heeded her own advice but knew Art had moved on. These days, with the Internet, it was hard to escape, and one night after too many wine coolers, she'd logged online and had found him, at a new job—one that specialized in building airplane wings. She'd written down the address and had driven there, hoping to see him. "When I was your age, my mom made me wear those types of shoes, too."

"She did? What did you look like when you were seven?" Kayla asked.

"A little like you. Shorter, though. My mom always made me wear dresses, which I hated because they were hard to play sports in. I loved basketball and riding my bike. Oh, and I always had my hair in braided pigtails. Do you ever wear your hair that way?"

"It hurts when my mom braids my hair."

"Really?"

"She pulls so hard. Why do they call them pigtails? They look like ropes."

"That's not catchy."

"What about pigropes?"

"Nope." Tiffany laughed. In this moment, Tiffany stared out of only *her* eyes instead of wondering how she looked to everyone else. At first, this sensation was purely mental, but later the feeling spread to her body: the pang in her hips faded, and the hard creases on her brow softened. "I can put your hair in braided pigtails—or 'pigropes'—if you like?"

"Do you wear your hair like that?"

"Not anymore," Tiffany said, gazing out the window, noticing that the sky's light had vanished. "They're too young. It'd be like me playing in a sandbox or swinging from monkey bars."

"I'm sleepy," Kayla added, yawning.

Tiffany trudged to the bathroom and, moments later, emerged with a comb and hair ties. She settled in behind Kayla. The girl's hair was silky, and Tiffany clutched a few strands, unsure of how to begin. As soon as she raked the comb through the girl's hair, instinct kicked in, and the process made sense. Tiffany divided the left side of the girl's part into three sections. She was careful not to work too close to the scalp, as she didn't want to repeat the same mistake as Kayla's mother. When one side was completed, she secured the braided pigtail with a hair tie. It looked nice. Relaxed and soft. Tiffany then repeated the same process on the other side. A few times, Kayla tried to turn her head toward the braid, but Tiffany told her to wait until she was finished.

"I need to see it!" Kayla said as Tiffany finished the other side.

"Just a second." Tiffany took to the bathroom, checking to see whether Kayla was moving, but the girl stayed still on the ottoman. Tiffany dug through her bathroom cabinets, searching for her hand mirror. She spotted it deep in a drawer, under some cotton swabs and a half-used tube of zit cream. "Coming!" she called. "Coming!" She wiped the mirror's glass with a hand towel but was careful not to look into it herself, keeping the mirror in line with the floor.

After handing the mirror to Kayla, Tiffany stepped back and folded her arms. Kayla raised her chin, twisted her neck, and analyzed the style from all angles. "It's cool," Kayla finally said. "I like moving my head around and feeling them hit my face." She showed Tiffany what she meant. "Do you have a photo of what you looked like with pigtails?" Kayla set the mirror face down on the ottoman.

Tiffany plucked a burgundy photo album off the mantel. She sat down beside the girl. In another life, she had enjoyed putting together these scrapbooks on Saturday mornings, but since her split with Art and the invention of the smart phone, there was really no need for such a thing. Photographs nowadays were so easy to take, delete, alter, and ignore. Never had people snapped more and seen less. With the album on her lap, she scooted close enough to Kayla to pick up traces of grape juice on the girl's breath. She flipped the heavy plastic pages and saw herself in a tire swing, wearing a Lakers T-shirt. And there she was, too, draped in a bedsheet on Halloween, the mouth hole enormous because her father "didn't want her to suffocate."

"Is that you?" Kayla pointed at a photo of Tiffany blowing out nine candles jabbed into a chocolate cake.

"Yes." Tiffany didn't remember that moment at all—almost as though if it hadn't been recorded by a camera, the instant wouldn't have been real.

"Look!" Kayla said, pointing to a faded Polaroid near the bottom of the page. "Your hair! You're wearing pigtails . . . and you're standing near a pig!"

"I never thought of that . . ." Tiffany said. She did recall that trip to the petting zoo: the heavy smells and the way her father told her to keep her hand flat to feed the horses.

"Can I try braiding your hair?"

Tiffany didn't respond. "Oh, it's okay. That's really sweet of you."

"Please," Kayla said, bringing her hands together.

Tiffany begrudgingly agreed, sinking to the floor so that Kayla wouldn't have to reach up. She kept the album on her lap, perusing the pages and taking trips back in time. What she remembered most about her youth was that her default emotion was contentment. These days, happiness appeared, but it was rare. Like a SoCal rainstorm.

Kayla giggled as she tugged at Tiffany's head. Tiffany wondered why. Did her hair smell? Was it greasy? Too coarse? She shut her eyes, bit her lip, and felt heat flood her forehead. The little girl's fingers kept at it, though, and she didn't seem disgusted or scared. In fact, when Tiffany opened her eyes and peered Kayla's way, the little girl's lips curved into a smile. Tiffany drew a breath and savored the warmth transmitted by Kayla's touch. "It feels like you're doing a good job. I can tell you've got three strands there." Tiffany stared back at the album. The overhead light's rays bounced off the glossy photos, so Tiffany repositioned the book. On this particular page were memories of a trip she'd taken with Art to Philadelphia. As with any vacation to the City of Brotherly Love, the photos were predictable: cheesesteaks at Pat's, the Rocky statue, even a visit to

194

the Liberty Bell. Tiffany combed over each detail, then dragged her pointer finger across the famous crack in the bell's dome.

"I think I'm done," Kayla said, locating the hand mirror and holding it out for Tiffany to take a look.

"I'm sure it's great," Tiffany said, setting the mirror back down on the ottoman.

Kayla got up and plopped on the couch. "Sometimes, I dream about my uncle. This one time, we went hiking, and I fell on a cactus, and he helped me pick the spikes out of my leg. It was weird. Do you ever dream like that? Do you think my uncle will be okay?"

"I hope he will." Tiffany grabbed a blanket that had fallen to the floor and draped it over the girl. Outside, the night was thick with the sound of crickets pulsing in the background.

"You look pretty," Kayla said as Tiffany adjusted the blanket.

Tiffany nodded. She returned to the ottoman, where she picked up the album once again. After a few more pages of staring at Art's thick eyebrows and delicate complexion, she shut the scrapbook. She wished now that she hadn't driven to his work to see him. But she had. She'd waited in the lot in her new car, under a shedding jacaranda. He'd pulled out of his spot in his old Camaro, the one he'd spent thousands on. A new engine, a rebuilt transmission, and a top-of-the-line exhaust. She'd followed him to his home in San Luis Obispo, only a ten-minute drive from his office, and had parked a ways down the road. After he'd headed inside with a pile of mail in hand and a bag slung over his shoulder, Tiffany took her foot off the brake pedal and approached. His home was a long one-story place with windows running the length of the

195

entire facade. Near the center of the house, she spotted the 1950's scene—a woman meeting her man after work, planting a kiss on his lips, her red hair undulant and spilling toward her face. Tiffany didn't stay long, just moments more, to make sure her eyes were telling the truth. Were their years together just a ruse? She could accept that her marriage had failed, but it was his lie that had hurt more than his leaving.

It wasn't long before headlights whipped into Tiffany's driveway, startling her. She stood and felt blood spread to her limbs. Through the windows by the front door, she spotted Kayla's father, whose name she'd already forgotten, walking under the outdoor lights.

Tiffany hurried over and pulled the door open. "She just fell asleep," she whispered. "How is everything?"

He kept his voice high, and Tiffany was tempted to shush him. "Not good. He's in a coma, and the doctors don't seem too optimistic. Wasn't wearing his seatbelt." There was a long pause. "Thanks for asking, though." A bug fluttered near his face, and he shooed it with a quick swipe of his hand.

"I'm sorry," Tiffany said.

"I'll just scoop her up," Kayla's father said. He approached the couch, reached down, and worked his arms under Kayla. Soon after, she was positioned perfectly against his body, with her head propped over his right shoulder. Somehow, she was still sound asleep. "I hope she was okay," the father added.

"Oh, she's . . . lovely," Tiffany said.

"Good," he said, heading out the front door. As he lumbered back to the SUV, Tiffany stood on the stoop, entranced by the girl's sashaying pigtails.

Eventually, Tiffany returned inside and locked the front door. She drew the curtains and turned off the TV. She cleaned up as best she could: pushing the ottoman against the matching recliner, putting away the photo album, and dumping the bucket's contents into the trash. She later folded the throw blanket on the couch and tucked the hand mirror into her jeans pocket.

Once she was in her bedroom, she inspected the dark facade of Kayla's home. Maybe the girl had woken up by now, and her father had told her about her uncle, and she was asking questions, pleading for the answer to—"Will he ever wake up?"

Before turning in, Tiffany brushed her teeth and splashed cold water on her face. In time, she even yanked the hand mirror out from her jeans pocket. Before shoving it back into the crowded drawer, she flipped the smooth glass her way. Her fingers quivered, and her eyes tightened, but seconds later, she surrendered. She widened her gaze and soaked in her likeness, even ran her fingers over the fragile strands of her braided hair.

HIGHWAY 111

Even at 11:59 p.m., the heat still owned Palm Springs. Emile's shift had started a couple of hours earlier, and he sat in his taxicab, munching on some stale donut holes, waiting for dispatch to inform him of his next pickup. He tinkered with the radio and absorbed some mundane news: It was hot. The Dow had fallen. People weren't watching the Olympics.

Tired of the A/C, he rolled down his window and let the arid wind sweep across his face. Twelve years out here, and his brain still had a hard time associating night with warmth. Emile took a slug of coffee and popped in his last donut hole. He stared at the green-lit dashboard clock and studied the pulsing dots between the hours and minutes. He clenched his jaw and ground his molars.

Seconds later, it was midnight, July 30th.

Nothing, of course, had changed. Highway 111 was identical to moments prior: razor-sharp cacti flanking the road, lampposts casting yellow rays onto the black street, and bright gas stations and fast-food restaurants emitting their noxious stink. Once again, he glanced at the time. This day always hurt.

Dispatch crackled through, alerting him of a passenger. Emile grabbed the CB and depressed the switch. "The strip club?" he said.

Dispatch confirmed.

Emile punched the gas and rushed past banks, liquor stores, and delis. The roads were clear, with only the occasional car or cab. America was turning into one big strip mall. Emile always joked that it was as if he were driving on a treadmill, unable to tell one block from another. The faster he drove, the harder air came at him, and he savored the way it raced over his arms and rattled his eardrums. 12:02, the clock read. The pulsing dots steady and strong, like a heartbeat. Where was she right now? Was her hair long? Were her fingers clad with rings? What shade was her lipstick? How sweet was her perfume?

Cars jammed the parking lot of Bambi's Booby Trap, and Emile waited in the messy line, the back wheels of his cab hanging into the street. He dragged his eyes across the neon sign of a woman kicking one of her legs high above her head. The sign was constructed in three parts: the first was a woman standing naturally, wearing cowboy boots, denim shorts, and a low-cut T-shirt; the second showed her kicking up halfway; and the last showcased her leg up by her head. Emile followed the sign through its progression before a parking lot attendant yelled at him to pull up.

He jutted forward and popped a toothpick between his lips. A young woman and man staggered toward the cab, whipped the door open, and flung themselves into the back seat. They were dizzy with laughter and dragged more heat into the car. Booze permeated the cabin.

"Where to?" Emile asked.

"Head toward Indian Wells," the man said. His hair was buzzed, and his eyes were wrapped with Buddy Holly glasses. He slammed the door, and Emile nodded and drove.

The young woman flicked on the overhead light and dug through her purse. Emile peeked in the rearview mirror, allowing his eyes to roam the woman. She was tight against her door, bursts of breath fogging up the window. She was attractive, around twenty, wearing a black-haired bob and a red tank top.

Large hoop earrings dangled from her lobes and swayed whenever the road roughened.

Dispatch asked whether Emile had picked up the client, and he confirmed.

"I like your accent," the young woman said. "Is it French?"

"Yes," Emile said.

"How long have you been here? In the US? In Palm Springs?"

"Too long."

"I've always wanted to go to France," she said. "Always wanted to walk the cobblestone streets. Are you from Paris?"

"Jesus, baby, leave the man alone. He doesn't need you breathing down his neck, okay?"

"Shut up," she said. "You're such an ass when you drink."

"Don't talk to me like that, all right?" the man said.

Emile glanced in the rearview and noticed the man's hairy hand resting on the girl's shoulder. The man then reached up and turned off the cabin light.

"It's fine," Emile said. "I don't mind. No, I'm not from Paris. I'm from Corsica, a little leaf-shaped island in the Mediterranean."

"Do you guys have cobblestones?"

"In important places."

At least twice a day, Emile withstood this conversation. Most of the time, he wished he was American so that people wouldn't have access to such an easy topic of conversation, but with this girl, he didn't mind. He liked her delicate voice, and he had the feeling that speaking with him was the farthest she'd ever traveled.

"You wanna know something?" she said.

"Will you shut up for a second?" the man said. "You wanna marry this man or something? You wanna have his babies? Damn!"

Emile turned on the overhead light and swung his head around. "It's fine," he said. "Okay? Let her be."

The man licked his teeth, and Emile peered down to see the man's thick hand on the young woman's knee. He was rough on her skin, not caressing but gripping and kneading.

"So, yes," Emile said, "I do want to know something." He clicked off the light, and blackness, once again, swallowed the cabin.

"Today's my twenty-first birthday."

"That's right," the man said. "No more fake IDs."

Emile's abdomen knotted, and his eyes burned. Obviously, he knew that people shared her birthday, but he'd never met another with it.

"Is that gonna get me a free ride?" she asked.

"Nope," Emile said. "Only an actual birth will do that."

"In that case," she said. There was some rustling in the back seat, and the girl began to spout impassioned moans. "Just kidding," she said.

"Don't play me like that," the man said. "Got me all excited."

"Whatever," the young woman said.

Emile remembered being her age. It was an easy time to sink back into. Back then, he thought he was invincible. All he cared about then was his Citroën and his Gitanes cigarettes. He'd only smoked them because of the design of the package: the silhouette of a seductive woman in a shroud of smolder.

He'd meet Françoise for lunch at the port, and they'd navigate her father's boat along the coastline, take in the calanques, and stop for a swim when the

202

heat became unbearable. Afterward, they'd share a towel and let the rest of their droplets dry in the sun. They'd savor a cigarette or two and do their best to construct interesting designs with their smoke. She'd often paint her toenails aboard the boat, and after some getting used to, Emile made his peace with the chemical smell.

"Hey, buddy, you ever been to that club?" the man asked.

"No," Emile said.

"Why not? You gay or something?"

"No, I just think a man should have to earn seeing breasts."

"Some beautiful girls in there, though," the man said.

"They were beautiful," the young woman said. "And they smelled so good. I just didn't like it when they clacked their heels together."

"I hope you go through with it," the man said to the young woman. "The manager really seemed interested. You got his number, right? Think of the loot you'll make."

"I don't know," the young woman said.

Emile cracked his toothpick and tossed it out the window.

"Strange to take your girlfriend to a strip club, don't you think?" Emile asked.

"What's strange is me listening to you run your mouth in your weird voice."

"Be quiet," the young woman said. "Calm down."

"Don't tell me to calm down. Shit. You know how much I hate that."

"You drank too much," she said.

Emile cranked the A/C higher. He then turned down the CB and covered the time, 12:18, with a wadded-up paper towel.

"You want one?" Emile heard the man ask.

"No, I told you before . . . I don't like 'em," she said.

Emile stopped at a red light and turned his head. A nearby Taco Bell lit the surroundings a pale shade of blue and allowed Emile to see into the back seat with ease. The man was holding a small baggy of what looked like pills.

"Not in my cab, okay?" Emile said.

"Relax, man."

Emile told the young woman to fasten her seatbelt.

The light flipped to green, and Emile accelerated.

The man did as he pleased—Emile knew he would—and popped some pills in his mouth and threw his head back. Emile swung his eyes over to meet the young woman's. Her mouth stayed tight in a flat line, and she offered a shrug. She then mouthed, "Sorry."

Emile nodded and drove hard. He loved being behind the wheel, in total control of the V-8, and he glided from lane to lane and watched the money grow on the meter. Up ahead, a green light turned yellow, and he punched the brakes and steadied the wheel. In a clothing store on the right side of 111, a mannequin stood tall under fluorescent lights. She wore a pink bikini and a large-brimmed straw hat. A tote bag dangled from her shoulder, too.

"Pretty lady," the young woman said. "Don't you think?"

Emile laughed. "Yes, very."

"Nice body, right?" she said. "Is she your type?"

204

"I guess. She doesn't have any hands. I feel like I need a woman with hands."

"Yeah, but this way you don't have to worry about getting slapped."

"What about dinner, though? It'd be hard to go out to eat."

"You could feed her. She could be your little baby," she said.

Emile clamped his teeth, and a bright pain spread through his gums. "Maybe," he said.

"Have you ever been to Paris?" she asked.

"Many times."

"So you've seen the Eiffel Tower?"

"Yeah."

"Have you climbed it?"

"No," Emile said.

The light changed, and again, Emile sped off.

"I'm a small-town guy," he said.

"How'd you end up in Palm Springs?" she asked.

"I came to California to get away, live by the beach, but it was too expensive, so a friend of mine helped me get a job out here."

A construction crew smoothed new asphalt with steamrollers, and a large sign with a flashing arrow directed drivers into a single lane. Emile rolled down his window and came to a stop. Flares hissed and glowed, and Emile stared at them until his eyes stung. Even when he turned away, he could still see the luster of their burn.

"Baby, just one," the man said.

"I've told you a hundred times that it makes me feel funny," she said. "You don't listen."

Emile wished he could tell the young woman not to take the stripper job—that most people thought they could do something for a little while and then change later in life, but life wasn't that convenient and easy to correct.

Emile turned on the radio, and Lou Reed's "Walk on the Wild Side" seeped from the speakers. He turned it up a touch. He muttered along as best he could, the lyrics snatched by the V-8's growl. Then the young woman joined in for a verse. When the saxophone came into play, Emile hummed and glanced in the rearview mirror, but it was too dark to see her expression.

"I love this song," she said.

"I like the way it makes me feel," Emile said, continuing to sing.

"You really know the lyrics," the young woman said.

"I learned English from Lou Reed and Bob Dylan and some from Elvis."

"I like the way you say Elvis, like *El-Veese.*"

"Thank you," Emile said.

She giggled.

The construction crew's orange vests lit up as the taxi's headlights brushed over the reflective material. A man held up a sign that said SLOW, and the single lane spread back into three.

When Emile was the girl's age, he thought love came easy. Even at the time, he knew it wasn't right to think such a thing, but he was young and handsome; his stomach was ribbed with muscles; his hair was thick; his jokes were funny. But now, thirty years later, he knew with certainty that Françoise was the only woman he'd ever loved. And sometimes, he'd swim in the thickness of old memories: feel her hot breath against his neck and inhale the olive oil of her soap.

"Just one. Come on," the man said. His voice was sharp. "You'll see. You'll feel good. Trust me."

Emile knew the man wasn't wearing his seatbelt and that the girl was, so he made sure no one was behind him and crushed the brakes. The tires squealed, and the steering wheel rattled under his grip. The man jolted forward, and his forehead slammed the thick plastic divider.

"Listen," Emile said. "She's said no twenty times. Are you stupid or something?"

"Shit," the man said.

"Sir, sir," the young woman said. "Stop. It's okay."

She reached through the opening in the divider and touched Emile on the shoulder. He let out a breath, pulled over, and threw the cab into Park.

His mind whirled. It was the first day of autumn, 1970. Church bells clanged in the distance, and sun sliced through flaking shutters. He only had a week before his obligated eighteen months of military service, and he spent as much time with Françoise as possible. They'd planned to sleep together for the first time at her parents' home. Her parents had left for Bastia to meet up with old friends. Françoise was flat on her bed, nude, her knees up. They took their time, giggled, and heard the mattress squeak with each thrust.

"What is your problem, dude?" the man said.

Emile's chest heaved, and he turned on the overhead light and faced the man. He started to speak but caught the girl's eyes. She seemed scared, with her palms facing forward, and a clammy sheen spread over her skin. "He gets like this when he drinks," she said. "He doesn't mean it. Really."

"Here!" the man said. "I'm having one more! See? See?" He dug into his pocket, rubbed a green pill between his fingers, and popped it into his mouth.

"No!" the young woman said.

207

"Why are you with this man, this loser?" Emile said.

"Don't judge me. Don't judge us. Just drive," she said. "Please, just drive!"

Emile's hands shook, and heat seized his chest and flashed up to his throat. He put the car in gear and took off, the needle swinging from thirty to forty to fifty.

Françoise's parents had come home early—of course they had—and found them coiled under thin sheets. Her father, a stocky man with a mustache, had struck Emile in the face repeatedly till his face had turned scarlet and his nose had been cracked in three places. To this day, the white of his left eye was stained with a fleck of blood that had never faded as the doctors had said it would.

Emile activated the cruise control and sailed straight through four intersections. The man in the back seat breathed hard, and the young woman consoled him with soft words.

"We're getting close," the young woman said to Emile. "Just keep heading straight."

Emile nodded. The steady stream of A/C dried the sweat on his face. His pulse stayed high, though. He heard the man say something about how sorry he was and how life was short. Emile didn't say a thing, but he disagreed: Life was long. Long as this highway. And a person was lucky when they finally ran out of gas. He slugged the final ounce of his coffee. It was sweeter than the rest had been, and he crunched on a few of the sugar granules.

"It's okay. It's okay. You're okay." The young woman tended to her man.

Emile felt a pang of worry for the girl. Soft murmurs hovered his way as she continued to console him. Emile made out the word *love* a few times, before turning up Janis Joplin. In five hours, his shift would end, and he'd drive home, pull into the carport of his trailer, and head inside. After a coldish shower, he'd throw some ground beef into a skillet and add whatever was in the fridge to liven it up: peppers, tomatoes, cheese. He'd wash it down with a cold one. Even though he was exhausted after his shift, he couldn't go straight to bed. He felt that if he went to sleep right away, the next day just began. Usually, he'd flip on the TV and catch an infomercial—something about juicers or knives or mattresses. He always enjoyed the opening minutes of the ads when they'd show a man or woman having trouble opening a can or hanging a picture, and the scene would be shot in black and white. Then, after "There has to be a better way!" was piped in, the product was introduced, and the screen morphed into color. Sometimes, the people became more attractive, too. If the infomercial didn't entertain him, he'd head outside and inhale the sky. Nothing could be compared to the desert night—no skyscrapers, no clouds, no pollution—and all those clusters of stars sparkling, flickering, all feeding the darkness their light.

"This is where it gets a little tricky," the woman said, leaning forward. "You have to make a right and then a quick left. After that, just take Saguaro all the way up."

"Okay," Emile said. His heartbeat had steadied, and he could no longer feel his pulse snap in his neck.

Maybe it was for the best. That's what he always told himself on this day, July 30th. After the beating, Françoise's father had demanded that Emile never see his daughter again, and he'd made sure of it, sending Françoise to an all-girls' boarding school in Normandy. The days were hard without anything to look forward to, even harder because Françoise never returned his letters. He could still recall scrawling "École des Roches" on postcards, envelopes, and packages, and waiting in line at the post office to buy the proper stamps. He'd always splurged for speedy service because he wanted to occupy her mind as soon and as often as possible.

"Just right here," the young woman said. "Right over there. That one."

"Nice place," Emile said, taking in the plain stucco house.

"We just rent the top part," she said.

Emile brought his window back up and shut off the meter, which read forty-two dollars. He opened his door, and the inside lights cut on. The girl dug through her purse, fed her hand through the divider, and offered fifty bucks.

The man had already left the cab and was standing up ahead, hunched. The taxi's headlights lit his body, making him seem pale and sick.

Just as the girl was getting out, Emile heard a splat. The girl had fallen hard face-first onto the road. Emile rushed to her side. Her hair was sprawled about the street, and the beep of the open driver's-side door kept time like a metronome.

"Are you okay? Miss? Are you all right?" Emile said.

Laughs flew from the man's mouth. "Shit," he said. "I could hear that from here. It was like, *thwack*!"

Emile hunched over and helped the young woman stand. He inspected her scraped palms and wadded the end of his T-shirt and wiped her hands clean. Emile stared back at the man who was still howling with laughter.

"High heels and rum," she said. "Not a great combination."

A thin rill of blood seeped from her chin, and Emile brought his head forward to get a better look.

"I'm okay," she said. "Seriously."

"What a lightweight," the man shouted. He staggered toward them with change rattling in his pockets.

"Can you not be an asshole? Just for a minute?" the young woman said.

"What did you say?" the man said. A crease ran hard between his eyebrows.

"I'm sorry," she said, angling her gaze toward the street.

"No," Emile said. "Don't be sorry." He shoved his arm in front of the girl and took a step toward the man.

"What the fuck is your problem, man? Leave us alone. Why can't you just be like other cab drivers and sit in your little yellow car and drive around?" The man's breath was hard with whiskey. "Now, baby, come here!"

Emile wouldn't let her move, though. His hand was tight around her wrist now, and she wasn't pulling very hard. He plunged his teeth into his lower lip.

A passenger had once told him the proper way to throw a punch: with the thumb wrapped around the outside, not tucked inside the palm.

Emile tightened his fingers and stared at the man. He swept over the man's large nose and patchy sideburns, inspecting the man's features until they no longer made sense—till they blurred into a messy configuration of hair and colors and skin.

Emile could see himself in the man's glasses, too, his face jaundiced by the streetlights. He cocked his arm back and brought his fist forward, but the man, even intoxicated, saw the punch coming.

The man ducked and came back up, blasting Emile across the jaw. Emile went down. His head smacked the concrete. His eyelids fluttered, and he took in the burn of the yellow streetlight above him, like a distant sun, the rays expanding and shrinking.

He shut his eyes. The young woman spoke to him.

He took a deep breath and listened to his heart whang against his ribs. He'd only received a single letter from Françoise, a thin one that he'd used as a bookmark for years in a dusty copy of Baudelaire's *Les Fleurs du Mal.*

"Emile," she'd written, "Thank you for all your letters. I have read them so many times that the paper now crinkles like money. I think it is best we no longer write and that we go our separate ways. Don't you think? It has been almost a year. After I left you, I became very sick. I thought it was heartbreak. And it was, but it was also something else—I was pregnant. I had to give the baby up. It was for the best. A child should not be brought into chaos. She was beautiful, though. I barely got to see her, but I can still remember how warm she smelled. She was born on July 30th. It rained here. I think I would have named her Lucie."

The young woman yelled at her man, told him to stop and to leave. The man continued to laugh. Heat from the concrete warmed Emile's back, and his thoughts swirled as the young woman's voice fluttered his way: "Hello? Sir? Are you okay? Sir? Sir?"

Emile's eyes snapped open, and this time, he spotted her face under the lamppost, a halo of orange light surrounding her dark hair. She extended her hand, and Emile reached toward her, gripping her fingers. After he was up, she leaned him against the side of the cab, and he caught his breath.

The man had left them behind and was trudging up the stairs to his place, still laughing, his hard footsteps thudding against the wood.

"Are you all right?" she said. "Are you okay? You're stronger than I thought."

Emile nodded. "Been in a few fights now, and I've still never landed a punch."

The girl traced Emile's jaw with her forefinger and dug through her purse. She pulled out a small pack of tissues and blotted his cheek. Blood saturated the thin paper, and she tossed it to the ground, where it lingered for a few moments before being stolen by the wind.

"You're going to tell me to leave him now, aren't you? That I could do better, right?"

Emile didn't answer.

"Things aren't always that simple," she said. "You know?"

Emile placed his fingertips against his right cheek and grimaced.

The young woman smiled at Emile, and the corners of her eyes creased. One front tooth was chipped, and he wondered how it had happened.

She looked up toward her place, and Emile's gaze followed. Red Christmas lights twinkled inside the window, and a few feet above the roofline bent the moon, in something of a horseshoe.

"Well," she said. "I better be getting inside now."

Emile patted the girl's shoulder and crossed his arms in front of his chest. "What's your name?" he asked.

"Sienna. Yours?"

"Emile."

She placed her hand between his shoulder blades and swished her fingers up and down on his T-shirt. "I'm so sorry," she said. "Really, I am."

"I am, too," he said.

Emile walked around to the driver's side and plopped onto his seat. He slammed the door, and the beeping finally stopped. He'd gotten so used to it that the sound still echoed in his head. Sienna took to the stairs, gripped the banister, and conquered each step, eventually reaching her second-floor home. Emile cracked the window. "Happy birthday," he said.

"*Merci,*" the girl said, offering a small wave.

Emile pulled away, giving himself time to make sure she got in safely. He could still smell her fleeting trace of mint dancing about the cab. Sienna, he thought. "Sienna," he said aloud. Then he put his window all the way down, turned on his rooftop light, and reset the meter.

OFFICE HOURS

Thom Clark sat in a holding cell in west Tennessee, a stark difference from his usual office at Memphis State, where he was chair of the English Department.

He stared at the floor and rubbed his bloodstained hands.

His cellmate, a man who had grunted when Thom had said hello minutes before, burped and rotated his neck, exposing a throat tattoo of Bugs Bunny smoking a cigarette.

***

Two weeks ago, Thom sat in his office, marking up students' papers, imploring his undergraduates to stop using banal phrases, like "soft as a baby's bottom" or "rising like a Phoenix," yet there he was, lamenting the fact that he'd slept with a student named Lane the night before, one from his Creative Writing 202 class. Talk about clichés.

Ever since his divorce, he'd been a mess, but he was too good at *pretending* to have it together. It had taken a divorce for him to realize that he was a fine actor, that he walked around in a constant role of "content professor," as if he were Daniel Day-Lewis in some indie film that critics adored.

Kathryn, his ex, was still—even a year later— the background on his computer screen. His DVR still recorded her shows, and sometimes he spritzed a few sprays of her lavender perfume on his sheets before bed.

She'd left him for a younger guy. And, as a result, Thom had done his best to try to "get younger":

he'd bought a vintage motorcycle (one he struggled to ride); he'd purchased band tees from an online site (some whose songs he didn't even know); and he'd gotten his hair dyed chestnut brown at a salon near Jackson (about an hour away from campus).

What made it worse for him was that he didn't do anything particularly wrong to let the relationship fall apart. No drinking. No abuse. She'd just slipped out of love. Some marriages died from gunshot wounds; others passed from old age.

A text came through on his phone. It was Lane: "Had fun last night. Let's do it again soon."

He thought Lane wanted more of a relationship. She'd mentioned going to see a play and visiting some wine bar in town. She'd added, too, that she would be done with school at the end of the year, and that they would no longer have to hide their affection. She'd actually used the word *affection*, which he thought seemed out of place for a woman who wore hot-pink underwear.

Thom rose and twisted the stick on the venetian blinds, allowing the shades to tilt and make the afternoon sun bearable. Afterward, he replied to some emails, mostly writing "Check your syllabus," and then made himself a cup of tea.

There was a knock at the door. The door was actually open, but students knocked anyway.

"Professor Clark?" the woman said. She was older than college age.

"Come in," Thom said, rolling up his sleeves.

The woman crossed the threshold of the door but didn't have a seat. Her face was plain, and her dark eyes were intense, complementing her black hair that was pulled into a loose braid. "You don't remember me, do you?" She took a seat and propped her purse on her knees.

217

"I'm sorry," he said. "So many students."

"Akari. I graduated ten years ago." She paused. "Wow, ten years ago. It feels crazy to say it. I was in your creative writing class my senior year and also in your French translation seminar."

"They cut that one. I loved teaching French translation. Maybe more than I enjoy teaching English, but the mother tongue pays the bills."

"Did I jog your memory?" she asked.

"A little," he said. "Akari." The name was unfamiliar enough that he thought he should remember her, but he didn't.

"I was sort of unremarkable." She crossed her legs. One of her wrists was heavy with bracelets, and they clashed as she wrung her hands.

"What did you write?" he asked.

"Love poems, mostly."

"Really?"

"Very short ones. A few lines . . ." She smiled. "You were always telling me I should expand, go deeper, unpack things. One time, though, you said something of mine reminded you of Neruda's."

"I'm sure I meant it." Thom hadn't broken eye contact with Akari in a while, so he did so now, blinking a few times, then pretending to search for something in one of his desk drawers.

"I know you did. That's why I liked you."

"Can I get you some tea or coffee?"

"I'm fine."

Thom wanted her to tell him what she was doing here, so he took a long sip of tea, hoping the silence would spur her to speak.

"I bet you're wondering what I'm doing here."

He nodded.

218

"It's a little funny, really. You see, after graduation, I went to grad school in Boston to become an architect . . ."

The sun beamed directly into Akari's eyes. Thom stood and adjusted the blinds once again.

Akari continued: "There, I met this Frenchman."

Thom nodded.

"It was wonderful, except that I fell in love with him, and he was married. We spent so much time together studying. It was just bound to happen, you know? Anyway, he and his wife separated, and I had an idea. I just remembered in class, one day, you talked about romance so well and how you and your wife wrote each other long love letters when she was working abroad for Habitat for Humanity . . . I think it was that, or maybe the Peace Corps."

"Wow, yes," Thom said.

"You spoke about love with such honesty, and I remember you saying something about how it was 'as vast and complex as the galaxies.' It always stuck with me."

"A little pretentious, no?" he said.

"It seemed heartfelt," Akari said.

Thom thought he should tell Akari that he and Kathryn were no longer a couple, but his face warmed from the praise, so he basked in the moment.

"I was wondering," she said, "now that Pierre has moved on from his wife . . . if you could help me with a love letter. I wrote a crummy draft, and you're the only man I know who wrote a collection of love poems and has translated French work." She took a breath.

Thom scratched his face.

"You aren't interested?"

"It's not that . . ."

219

Akari nodded.

Thom recognized that look—the one that said, "I have it together," when in reality, the face wanted to crumple.

"You're busy," she said. "It was silly. You ever think something's great until you do it? You hear the words, and you're just like, What the hell?" She opened her purse and pulled out some papers. "I've tried. I did what you said all those years ago: unpacked, told him how I felt. I just can't get the words down."

Thom finished his tea.

Akari continued: "Do you ever get the sense that if you just wrote the perfect line in the absolute perfect way, someone could love you?"

"The written word is nice that way. It can be groomed, you know?" He reflected more on her question. The oral word was so impulsive—nothing could be smoothed out, and the memory of poorly spoken words often haunted him.

"So," Akari said, "do you think you could help?"

Thom popped his knuckles. "Sure," he said.

***

Thom thought this was what happened when a good man tried to do bad: he botched it.

The photo had upset him, and he'd had some wine while cooking, and he'd been high on the old love letters.

He continued to wait for his phone call. The guards had told him he would get his turn in a matter of minutes.

***

Lane wore one of Thom's T-shirts that hung low on her body. She ate her eggs, and Thom ate his. She asked him about his classes, and he asked about hers. She smiled and nodded, and he did the same.

Relations with Lane were a sort of medicine: healthier than booze yet containing a more complicated hangover. But at least with her, he didn't think. It was the thinking that killed us more than anything else.

The reality of Kathryn's new boyfriend— Donnie, the pastry chef, the one she'd showcased on social media for the last eight months—sometimes drifted away when he stayed in the sheets with Lane, but there was little he could do to *permanently* avoid the reality that Kathryn was moving on.

He forked a couple of over-easy eggs and watched the yolks run. Maybe Donnie could slip in the shower, have a heart attack while jogging, or fall off a ladder while stringing Christmas lights. These sorts of miracles happened, right? They probably did, but they wouldn't happen for Thom. No, no. Thom would have to hope for the old-fashioned death—the one that came from years and years together only to discover that sustained love was as mythical as the Loch Ness Monster.

"Wanna grab lunch today?" Lane asked. "We could meet at your office?"

He blotted his lips with a napkin. "I have some meetings."

"Last night, you said you were free."

Yolks oozed across his plate. "Oh, yeah," he said. "It's tomorrow, I think. Why don't you swing by the office at noon?"

"Perfect. I'll bring some food from that new Korean spot."

"Yummy," he said, reflecting on his word choice.

***

Thom dialed Akari. The guards had given him access to his cell phone to peek at his numbers, and he knew that Akari would come pick him up and bail him out, too. He would pay her back right away.

"Leave one at the beep," Akari's message said, and Thom heeded the instructions: "Hey," he said. "I'm in jail. In a holding cell. Can you bail me out if you get this? I'll pay you back right away. I'm good for it." Then he hung up the phone hard, and one of the guards screamed to "take it easy."

Take it easy. That was bullshit advice for anything in life. It wasn't easy, and pretending it was made it harder. Take it normal. Why didn't we just say that?

***

In the bathroom catty-corner to his office, Thom washed his hands. A little plant, something of a fern, sat near the sink, and there was a sign propped on its pot that read, "If you wouldn't mind giving me a water from time to time, I'd appreciate it. —The Biology Department."

He was of two minds about this plant. If the bio department was so keen on keeping this fern alive, then they should have kept it in their offices and watered it. It wasn't the responsibility of the professors on the third floor of Johnson Hall to feed this plant. Then, other times, when Professor Clark was content with the world, he thought it was rather sweet that everyone did their part to keep the roots growing. He even liked that the note was written in first person.

When he returned to his office, he did some grading, pulling some essays from a huge stack. The pile teetered with every tug of paper, reminding him of how he used to play Jenga with Kathryn on Sunday nights before they opened a bottle of wine and watched HBO. The scenario played, details ripe and poignant: her laugh, her grape-stained teeth after too much merlot, her hair nestled against his shoulder.

Then he did the thing he'd been so good at avoiding: checking Instagram. Kathryn had posted six times since his last inspection. Two pics of her new rescue dog Clementine in a black-and-white filter. That didn't bother him much. A little, but not much. A few sunset photos for which the caption read, "Blessed." And then one with Donnie. The two of them, their feet propped on a leather ottoman, Clementine tucked between their socked feet.

Beads of perspiration sprouted around his hairline, and his lower back knotted.

"Hey!" Lane said, entering his office. She wore a jean shirt paired with jeans of a darker wash and carried a paper bag that was stained with food grease. Her smile beamed. He loved how physically perfect she was, how everything at her age was just so. Her face: creamy and smooth. Her hair: blond and thick. And her body: perky in the right spots, soft in others.

Thom shut off his computer monitor before rising to meet Lane. When he reached her, he closed the office door, turned the lock, and set the bag down on his desk. He pushed her hard against the wall and brought her arms over her head. With her wrists pinned, he kissed her on her neck, dragging his tongue over her collarbones. Lane scratched at the back of his neck. The image of Kathryn and Donnie's feet on the

223

ottoman faded as they moved quickly from kissing to undressing.

There was a knock at the door.

Thom ignored it, even though he and Lane stood only feet away from the sound.

The knock returned.

"Come back later," Thom said.

Again, the knock, louder this time.

"Come back later!"

"Professor Clark," the woman said. "It's me . . . Akari. You said to come by today at twelve thirty. When would you like me to return? Sorry if I'm bothering you."

"Akari?" Lane whispered into Thom's ear.

"Oh," he said. "Yes, yes. Give me five minutes. Wait down the hall on the red couch."

"Is everything okay?" Akari asked.

"Yes! Just go wait down the hall!"

"Okay," Akari said.

"Sorry," Thom said to Lane.

They didn't resume. The moment had vanished.

Thom explained to Lane that he couldn't do lunch after all, that he'd promised his time to Akari, which he now vividly remembered.

Lane sighed, opening the brown paper bag and giving him the kimchi burrito and Coke she'd ordered for him. "Well, we *almost* had fun."

"Ah, the title of my autobiography," Thom said.

Lane didn't answer.

***

Thom drank a cup of water—not really a cup, but one of those paper cones that a person couldn't set down—

224

and stared at his cellmate with the Bugs Bunny tattoo. "What'd you do?" Thom asked.

"Stabbed a man," he said. "Not the first time, either." He delivered the words matter-of-factly, as if he had run some errands. "Had to, you know? The world will push you around until you push back." He cleared his throat and hocked up some phlegm. "You?"

"Kinda lost it." Thom pointed to his bloodied hands.

"Kinda?" The man seemed irritated that Thom hadn't totally committed. "That's too bad."

***

Akari and Thom sat in his office.

"I'm sorry about knocking earlier," Akari said. She sported a blue corduroy blazer paired with fashionable khakis. "You said you might have something for me today. A little draft?"

"I'll get to it tonight," he said.

"I'm just worried. I mean, by the time you get it to me, I have to write it in my handwriting and get to a post office. And then it has to go from Tennessee to France . . . Who knows how long that'll take?"

He clicked on his computer monitor, and Kathryn's Instagram once again seized the screen. The photo of the feet. The same feet that used to be in *his* bed, *his* shower—the same feet that used to stroll with *him* along the damp banks of the Mississippi.

"Are you okay, Professor Clark?"

"Yes," he said, but her gaze told him she didn't buy it.

"It doesn't have to be long, but it does have to be good."

"I know." He closed the window on his computer screen. He didn't want to be alone tonight,

225

nor did he want to be with Lane. "Would you like to come to my place for dinner? We could work on the letter together."

"Do you think the answer will be positive, Professor Clark?"

"It's funny how love turns everyone into a nervous thirteen-year-old."

"Yeah."

"But rejection heals. Regret festers," he said.

She nodded and gave him her cell number. They then squared away the details before saying their goodbyes.

Thom walked home.

That day, like every Thursday, a farmers' market was set up on campus, so Thom picked out a couple of items for his evening with Akari: olive bread and a few blood oranges.

It wasn't long before he was home, defrosting a chicken in the microwave and snapping the stems off of some green beans. When the bird was thawed, he took his time with it, placing some carrots and potatoes under its body so that the poultry wouldn't burn against the steel. His mind and body went through the same routines that they used to when he was with Kathryn: rushing home to cook in an attempt to surprise her, hoping the aromas would grow fast enough to wrap her when she entered from a long day at work.

Before long, Thom did what he'd been avoiding and opened the door to the basement. He descended the creaky steps and reached the box in the cobwebby corner. He brought it to the dining room, where he could go over its contents with Akari this evening.

He checked on the chicken and then returned to the box and opened the cardboard flaps. Inside were dozens of postcards from all over the world due to

Kathryn's job—right out of undergrad—at Habitat for Humanity. She expressed sincere tenderness in such few lines, and even though Thom was the author whose walls were plastered with degrees, she was always the one with the right words.

Thom raked his hand through his hair and sat down, inspecting her sentences:

So hard to experience all this beauty when we are rivers, ranges, and time zones apart.

I look at the moon and find peace in knowing that you see the same one.

I keep thinking about your mom's passing. I see her in you all the time. The lines around your eyes, your fingernails, your smile. Her DNA will always be the best part of you.

Love has made me corny: you are the love of my life.

Thom imagined Kathryn's fingers near these words, a pen in her grip, the careful dotting of her *i*'s, the intricate curves of her *y*'s. At one point, she cared enough to write every day, and he riffled through the box and found more letters. On some of them, she had scrawled on the front and back, making the papers crinkly. His face warmed, knowing that he was once the man who occupied her thoughts in baths, taxis, and those soft seconds before dreaming.

Time passed quickly reading over Kathryn's sentences, paragraphs, and pages, and before long, it was almost time for Akari's arrival. He grabbed some Post-its. As much as he railed against plagiarism, even expelling a student for it years ago, he would never be able to come up with lines as powerful as these. Her

227

words had to be harvested, so he lifted some of her most fragile sentences, wrote them on various Post-its, and shoved them into his jacket pocket.

Thom hurried now, setting the table, opening a bottle of wine, and retrieving the chicken from the oven. Garlic wafted across the kitchen, and in time, he sliced the bird and divvied up the dark and white meat. Then he pulled out the loot from the farmers' market and scattered the blood oranges and olive bread on a cheese board.

The sight of the box made his chest tighten. He wanted to see her face, the delicate strands of her hair that always tickled her forehead, and her mole to the southeast of her lip—so he pulled out his phone and checked out her Instagram.

A new photo shined, one from minutes earlier: her and Donnie at Sage, a nearby fancy restaurant. Nice clothes, toothpaste-commercial smiles, and a hot bread basket between them. The caption read "#LoveOfMyLife."

There was Donnie—in a white shirt buttoned all the way to the top, no tie. One of his large hands wrapped the stem of a wineglass while the other draped Kathryn's fingers.

Thom rose. He started moving. He had to leave.

Pain seized his body, and he sort of sleepwalked to his car, started it, and began driving toward Sage. The trees and road signs blurred as he accelerated.

Maybe if Thom's pain *really* confronted its source—and he could see her, see him, in real life—the healing process would finally begin.

The tires screamed as he whipped into the lot, and he nearly struck a pedestrian. He threw the car into Park and hopped out. Breath after breath hissed

228

through his nostrils as he trudged to the front door of the restaurant. Christmas lights, even though it was October, hung under a green awning, and he stood in their warm glow before bringing his face to a window.

Donnie and Kathryn laughed, and Thom watched Donnie's mouth move and move. He seemingly told a story that infatuated Kathryn. She laughed and covered her face, as she always did, with her fingers splayed over her mouth.

Love of my life, Thom thought.

He grabbed hold of the door handle, felt the cold steel against his palm, and opened the door a sliver, just enough for a bit of warmth from the dining room to funnel toward his face.

He saw them, heard them better, and stopped, unsure of what he'd do when he arrived at the table. He let go and allowed the door to fall back flush with the threshold, where it clicked softly into place.

Back in the parking lot, he spotted Donnie's SUV. He knew it was Donnie's because Thom had driven by Kathryn's place a couple of times and seen the green Ford Explorer on her driveway. Inside, a bouquet of carnations rested on the passenger seat.

Thom envisioned the next few hours: they would share a dessert, leave Sage hand in hand, and enter the SUV. Donnie would turn up the heat and the radio, and they would laugh the laughs of a deliciously exhausting evening. Then, Donnie and Kathryn would return home, prop their feet up, have some more wine, and he would kiss her below her earlobe, her sweet spot, and she would sigh. The sigh would lead to more heavy breaths, and the rest was as predictable as sunrise.

Thom's neck tensed. He rubbed his face and stared at his reflection in the driver's-side window, examining his puffy eyes, receding hairline, and pale skin before yanking the sleeve of his coat over his fist in one hard tug, until it wrapped his knuckles; then, in one swift motion, he slammed his hand into the driver's-side window.

The glass didn't break, but dozens of small cracks formed and held the window together.

Again, he punched. More cracks.

Once more.

This time, it gave, and shards of all sizes poured onto the driver's seat. The sound, a breaking and giving, healed him.

Thom struck again, this time, bashing one of the rear windows. He continued his work, wishing Donnie owned a limousine so he could pummel more glass. The same smashing on every window took place until the car looked like an abandoned building. Afterward, he took heavy breaths and strolled the perimeter of the vehicle to inspect his work.

He stood in the cold, watching his exhales form long plumes of smoke.

Moments later, he heard a siren.

***

"Thom Clark?" an officer said. "No charges were filed. You're free to go. Looks like your ride is here, too."

Akari sat on a bench near the door, and Thom walked toward her, nodded, and profusely thanked her for coming. He couldn't believe Kathryn and Donnie had decided not to press charges, and it made him feel worse in a way, as if they took pity on him instead of hating him.

"Can I take you home?" Akari asked.

"Please," he said.

He sat in the passenger seat, listening to the radio play and the heater blow. The volume on the stereo was too low to pick up on any specifics of the music, but it might have been something by Bach.

"I won't ask," she said.

Thom nodded. He felt comfortable in Akari's car, watching her make turn after turn, the cones of her headlights illuminating the dark road ahead and tossing light onto blackness.

She offered Thom a stick of gum, and he enjoyed the minty burst, especially after accidentally biting his cheek while punching out the windows on the SUV.

Thom shoved the gum wrapper into his jacket pocket, and his fingers encountered the edges of the Posts-its from earlier, their pale-yellow bodies tattooed with romance. He grabbed them, lowered the passenger-side window, and opened his palm. The scraps of confetti fell and fluttered into the cold night, and he tracked their dance for a few seconds in the side mirror.

Afterward, he put the window back up, angled the heating vents toward his face, and pictured the chicken that he'd made, sitting in the center of the set table, waiting, its body no longer coiling with steam.

REMMY

For Sophfronia

I know we're not popular right now. We guns have had our moments. Had a lot of 'em for a long time, actually. But really, you see, we're just a bunch of parts. Like anything else you use—like your fancy refrigerators, cars, or those phones you all seem so obsessed with. But even though we're just an assemblage of steel and welded units, everything has a soul. I know that. Everything comes from the earth in some way, so it's very much alive.

I have loved a boy all of my life, only belonged to him. It was in the summer of 2006 that I was purchased for Jasper.

Jasper's uncle, Leroy, bought me at a gun show, a simple .22 rifle. I had been previously owned by a member of the Crow tribe in southern Montana, about a hundred miles from where I live now. I was never used by that man, but he was kind, and peaceful, and preferred to hunt for deer with a crossbow.

Leroy gave me to Jasper on his seventh birthday. He didn't like me at first. He was scared to hold me. I could feel his little, soft hands on my trigger and stock, and he held me like he was afraid to break me. Then, though, little by little, when he came over to Leroy's house, he would ask to hold me, and Leroy would take me down from the high shelf in the closet and tell Jasper how to position me and to be sure never to point my barrel in the direction of anyone, even if I wasn't loaded. I was almost never loaded.

Jasper's grip got stronger and stronger, and before long—I would say by the age of nine—he was holding me like he knew what he was doing.

From my place, high in the closet, I would watch him draw, paint, play with toy trucks, yo-yos, footballs, action figures, and sports cards. I was always over him.

Sometimes, too, Leroy would make Jasper get used to me in the most significant way—by actually shooting me. Leroy thought it might scare Jasper to bring me to the range because of all the people and noise; besides, out here in rural Montana, there's so much acreage that everything could be considered a range of some sort. So Leroy and Jasper would pack up the baby-blue truck, put me and the gear in the rusty bed, and head out west near the foothills.

The sky matched the truck's hue—that perfect shade, and I remember the fragile air scraping over me, the ideal temperature. And the tops of trees that hovered over the truck, blending into one long green swath.

Once we arrived at Leroy's spot, he put out some old pumpkins, bottles, cans, and target sheets. After showing Jasper how to fire, Leroy had Jasper give it a go. It was our first shot together.

Leroy backed away, gave the boy space. And Jasper placed my stock against his tiny shoulder. I could tell he didn't want to disappoint his uncle as he checked off each of the steps Leroy had taught him: stock firm, line up sight, deep breath, squeeze trigger. He lined me up on an old Coke bottle and whispered, "Okay, Remmy. Help me with this." He dug his boots into the soft dirt and calmed himself with big breaths. Little by little, he steadied me and focused on his target. The bottle glinted in the afternoon sun, a big star of light just right above the red label. "Okay, Remmy," Jasper said again.

And he squeezed my trigger.

The bullet sliced through my body at thousands of feet per second and escaped into the cold air, hitting the bottle right at the base.

The shards glittered and reflected light before settling onto the ground. It all happened so fast. I could hear Jasper's breath, even feel his hot exhales as he lifted me and pointed me up, my body close to his mouth. He didn't want to hurt a thing, and like I said before, everything has a soul, and I think he felt that. I knew he felt that, and I knew he was sad for what he did to that Coke bottle. But he didn't want to disappoint Leroy.

They shot more that day, and Leroy was impressed with the boy's abilities.

Leroy and his wife, Faith, were divorced. They had tried for a kid of their own but had to stop when the doctor told them Leroy couldn't—something about his injury from the Gulf War.

I knew Leroy blamed himself for the divorce. I even heard him say to his friend one night that "a real man would've been able to give his wife children," so I guessed that when Jasper came over, Leroy was happy he got to play dad and pretend that Faith was visiting her mom or delayed at the airport. With certain edits, Leroy could feel like he had it all.

The truck rides were my favorite. Sure, I was designed to be held and fired, but I liked company, too, and sometimes, after Jasper would shoot me at "the range," he would decide to ride in the back of the pickup with me. There, I would rest at his feet, and we would take in the world. There's a reason they call Montana the Big Sky State.

Sometimes, he would lie down with me in the rusty bed and line his eyes up with nothing but blue. There, we were protected a bit from the elements— just enough to feel like we were inside, with all the metal surrounding us, but also, clearly outside, with all that fresh air and those white clouds that seemed thick enough to walk across. Jasper would poke them sometimes, and he would compare them to real things. One time, he saw one that looked like a handgun with little bullets popping from its barrel. Another time, he saw an elephant with this gigantic curly trunk, and he traced his small finger over it and laughed and laughed. I guess clouds were to him what his freckles were to me—something otherworldly that captivated.

In the fall of 2008, we had our first hunt. Deer. Jasper had gotten used to me, used to holding me, feeling my weight, my barrel, but for the both of us, it was the first time we were going to kill. Leroy was a good teacher—and he kept the boy feeling strong.

The fall of 2008 was also a tough time for Jasper personally. He cried a lot after he hung up the phone with his mother. He said things like, "Do you know how long Dad will be locked up for?" and "Do you think we will be able to visit?" His mother's voice was loud on the other end of the phone. She wasn't all that kind to Jasper, not as nurturing as I hoped she'd be. A couple of times, she even snapped and told him to pull himself together and that it was "good for him" and that "he needed to be put away." Jasper placed the phone back in its cradle, and ran the back of his hand over his eyes, and looked at himself in the full-length mirror near my perch. He didn't want Leroy to see that he had cried. He made sure his blue eyes were nice and dry before heading back into the hall.

The man who had me before Leroy and Jasper never wanted to show pain, either. It must be hard for humans to always pretend to be strong. I guess I have the same issue. People see a gun, and they only see the pain I can inflict; they don't see anything else.

Anyway, it was a few hours after that phone call that we went on the first real hunt. And I could feel a difference in Jasper's grip. It was firm and strong, confident even. He knew what I was and what he could do with me.

It was a fall day that pretended to be winter. Leroy and Jasper's boots squeaked through the snow, leaving four footprints in our wake—one pair a size twelve, one pair a size six and a half. Wind whipped, stirring up tornadoes of fresh powder that pummeled us, and sometimes, Jasper and Leroy would turn their backs to the force in order to keep their eyes protected. It was a long slog, the trees swaying with each haymaker sent from mother earth, but eventually, with little steps up the side of the mountain, we made it to a place where the views were open, and we could see down into a little valley flanked by thick clusters of pines that shielded many of the deer, according to Leroy.

Leroy squinted and turned up his voice to combat the wind: "The bucks, the deer, they stay in their little tree cocoon. But eventually, when the wind dies down, the deer have eaten all they can in that area, and they'll venture out toward the valley, and they'll keep their heads low."

Jasper nodded. I thought the nerves would come and that I'd feel his hands begin to tremble, but he rested easy with my body positioned diagonally against his chest. His heartbeat was a steady rhythm that ticked like a clock; his breath, the rise and sink of his inhales and exhales, flowed steady and harmonious.

When a buck came into sight, the world went still. All other senses but sight were silenced, muted, and the world, even on this harsh day, became peaceful in a way—just stirs of powder and branches thick with snow bobbing up and down. "Let him come closer," Leroy said. "Be patient."

I was pointed at the valley, and we remained motionless.

Minutes passed. Long minutes, thick with cold.

Then, the buck with perfect antlers walked directly into the valley, stopped, looked up, and then returned his head to the ground in search of some grass underneath the powder. He pushed the snow around with his snout, clearing a large patch, and then munched on some blades.

Leroy turned to Jasper and gave him a nod. They had gone over the specifics of this moment many times, and I wanted the best for Jasper. I really did. The boy had been through a great deal: his mother being tough and his father being sent away, and all he really had was his uncle and these weekend getaways; plus, who really knew why his mom was sending him to Leroy's to begin with? Who really knew what she was up to? So I whispered something of a prayer for Jasper.

Leroy nodded again as if to say, "Hurry up." His eyes widened, too. Traces of snow rested on the tops of his eyelids and frosted on his eyebrows as well.

Jasper didn't take long. He worked through the checklist just like he had that day in the foothills, and before long, I could feel his finger take my trigger.

He tracked the animal, adjusted for the wind, and with a quick squeeze, I did my job, blasting a shell at the buck.

The buck heard the blast, but by the time it looked up, the bullet struck its flank in a blow that took the buck down. Powder splashed around its frame. Leroy fired to make sure. Then fired again.

Three large cracks in a row, and then a long exhale from Jasper.

The world regained its way, and Jasper smiled. I hadn't seen him sport a grin—a large one where his lips parted, and his teeth shone—in months.

I was surprised to see him smile. Only a couple of years ago, he nearly cried when the Coke bottle exploded, but maybe because he was closer, maybe because the sound was more immediate.

As we trudged down the hillside thick with snow, the buck came into view. Blood was seeping across its pelt and into the powder. "Looks like a cherry snow cone," Leroy said, and Jasper nodded.

The boy didn't seem upset by the slain animal. He placed his hand on the buck's back, a place where the blood hadn't run, and seemed proud of his work. He didn't speak. He didn't breathe hard.

"A hell of a shot, J," Leroy said. "That time we put in really paid off, but it's always hard to simulate game-time conditions."

Jasper nodded. He stroked the buck's pelt, first with the grain, then against it. Then Leroy detailed what to do with an animal after it was killed. He said it was the hard part, the gross part, the reason most people went to the supermarket and walked down aisles, to see meat already trimmed, behind thick glass, in rows divided by sprigs of parsley. Jasper was to stay with the animal while Leroy walked back to the house to get the truck.

Jasper kept his wits about him—*wits* was the word Leroy had used—and Jasper did as he was told. He shifted his body to scan his surroundings, making sure no animals came for the meat. It was rare, but sometimes if a carcass was left like this out in the snow for a while, other predators—bears mostly in these parts—would venture out for an easy meal.

239

There was a pride to Jasper. Everything in his life seemed out of his control. People say, "Don't worry about what you can't control." But that's never made much sense to me—of course you worry about what you can't control. Death. Money. Love. Because those things are stressful, and those things are worrisome. Who worries about things they can control? Bedtime, shoe-tying, breakfast. No one. And the same went for Jasper. He couldn't control school, his family, friends, but hunting with Leroy was a way in which he could tame the world, even take a life, and that was power at its finest.

Months passed without another hunt because Leroy only hunted when he needed food. He had killed an elk and a deer, then carved them up, and frozen the meat in an industrial-sized freezer that he kept in the garage. Most nights, he would cook up a small chunk of meat from the freezer and mix it with a can of beans. "Healthy and cheap," he always said.

I now rested proudly on a rack in the guest bedroom, unloaded of course, but it was nicer, and I had better views of the room where Jasper would stay when he came out to see Leroy and me. His frequency increased, too, and sometimes he would stay for the whole week, and Leroy would have to call the bus driver and let her know that Jasper was living out with us for the week. She seemed easy to talk to and always agreed to pick him up.

On Jasper's thirteenth birthday, he was alone in the house. He was supposed to go for a little hike on this mid-March day where the sky was open and clear and the sun sliced right into the guest bedroom and warmed my stock and barrel. (He had invited his girlfriend, Fiona, at the time, but how serious can a thirteen-year-old girlfriend even be?) She called often, and Leroy would call out from the other room, "It's

240

that girl again." And Jasper would answer, "Cool! I'll take it in my room." Jasper still didn't have a cell phone. His mom wouldn't get him one. She said it was because she wanted "to keep him innocent for as long as possible," but Jasper thought that it was just a poetic way of saying she was cheap.

Fiona called that day, his birthday, as he rested on the bed, doodling in a leather-bound sketchbook that Leroy had bought for him at some shop in town. He liked to draw. And he did so often.

Through the receiver, Fiona's voice was high, and her laugh was higher. She talked a lot, and Jasper drew and drew, his left hand sketching and sketching, the base of his hand turning the color of steel from accidentally smearing all the pencil graphite.

The line went flat for a while with neither of them bringing up a new topic. Just then, though, Jasper asked when she was coming over to hang out, that Leroy had planned a little something, that he was buying a cake, and that they would all play cards, and that a neighbor had promised him to let them ride horses.

"Oh," Fiona said. "That sounds nice." But she didn't say anything else.

"So," Jasper added. "In a couple hours?"

She didn't say much more. She called him "amazing" and "sweet" and "incredible." His face whitened, and he shut his eyes as if expecting pain to come. He sometimes did the same thing when his mom would call and chat with him on the phone.

When he started to cry, he brought the phone away from his ear and placed it face down against his red quilt.

After hanging up the phone, he came for me, yanking me off the rack and rushing to the garage to load me. He stuffed some extra shells in his pockets, too.

We hurried out back. In the distance was a busted tractor, and Jasper fired and fired at the rusty metal, the rounds dinging against the steel over and over. His rage seemed soothed by the blasts, so he fired more and more rounds, never once missing the target. Then he collapsed to the ground and flung me far into the distance.

From there, I watched his body heave as he sobbed. I wished I could console him. I wished that someone would. But Leroy was on the other side of town, picking up the cake, and there was nothing I could do but lie there, some twenty feet away, still warm from all the gunfire.

I stayed outside for two weeks, actually, until Leroy found me while chopping firewood. He had a stern talk with Jasper about gun safety. It felt good to be in the warm house again on the rack in the guest bedroom, where I could see Jasper and feel like something of an angel, looking over him as he slept the sleep of a teenage boy.

It only got harder for Jasper. Only a few months after his birthday, I found out through conversations between him and Leroy that Jasper's mom was arrested for meth possession while driving home from her secretarial job. She claimed the paraphernalia wasn't hers, that it belonged to someone at work, that she didn't even know it was in the car. She was sentenced to six months in jail—a light amount for the offense— followed by time at a recovery clinic per the judge's orders.

At night, Jasper would kneel bedside and pray. I had never seen him do this before in all his time with me. I mean, sure, he'd ask me to help him shoot straight when he was learning how to fire all those years ago, but this was the first time he'd gotten religious, and he would sometimes press his face into his pillow and scream. I hoped life would give him a break. I hoped whatever he was praying for wouldn't wait years to show up.

During that time, Jasper stayed at Leroy's. I couldn't see them, but I could hear them, and they didn't talk much. It was a lot of TV and homework, a lot of doodling, too, on a big pad. Sometimes, Jasper wouldn't like what he drew, and he would just toss the large pieces of paper to the foot of his bed, where they would strike the closet door before falling to the carpet. I would get a peek. Lots of bullets flying from guns, and knives, and cowboys, and crosses.

A couple of times, when Leroy was still at work, Jasper would bring girls from school over to the house, and they would fool around on the bed. When he was nearly sixteen, he had sex for the first time. It didn't last long, and the girl seemed to be in pain, but Jasper was nice and asked her if she was okay a lot. She had long red hair and skin that was so pale her thighs blended in with the sheets.

He wanted to see his folks, but Leroy never took him, said it would be too hard to see them like that, and Jasper just nodded. It seemed to me that Jasper and Leroy did better when the relationship was uncle and nephew, and now that Leroy had to be there all the time, it got to be too much. He wasn't the wise, cool uncle any longer, and that was a role that Leroy relished. Instead, he too was a sort of absent father, working a lot, and doing his best to keep the boy afloat. But afloat is no way to live.

Leroy clearly felt bad for the kid, buying him new shirts and even a bottle of cologne once, but it seemed Jasper's sadness couldn't be derailed. He kept a stoic face most of the time, one that seemed numb, except in his bedroom, where Jasper was up at all hours of the night, crying and sweating and praying and cursing out God. "If you're real," he said one night, "then why the fuck are you allowing all this shit to happen? What did I do?"

He kept having sex with the pale girl. Most of the time, that's all they did. Sometimes, they took pills from a little orange bottle she kept in her backpack. Sometimes, they drank from a green water bottle. They almost never talked or shared anything other than stupid jokes. One time, Jasper got quiet and said, "I really like you. Do you like me?"

She waited and then laughed.

Then Jasper laughed, too, and said, "That was a good one, right?"

And she said, "Hilarious." Then dropped back on the bed.

They spent hours like this, comforted by nothing more than another body in the room.

***

Hunting seasons would come and go. Looking out the window, I could tell just by the light that the seasons were changing and that I wasn't going to be used yet again. It saddened me. I didn't feel useful. All things need to be used. Without use, we just die with open eyes.

Then one day, Jasper came home crying. A perfect black-and-blue crescent moon hung under his swollen left eye. He chucked his backpack hard into the wall.

Books tumbled from it. Pens sloshed. He stared hard at himself in the mirror beneath me. He pushed his tongue around his closed mouth. I waited to gain some sort of context, but it never came.

Leroy entered the home a couple of hours later, and their voices blended with the sounds of the television and the microwave that just kept beeping and beeping. Leroy said, "I'm sorry" twice, but I couldn't learn much from that. "Let's get away from it all," Leroy then said. "Maybe a little camping trip. I can ask a guy from work for his camper. Maybe some fishing, too. Even hunting." I perked up at the idea of being held in Jasper's hands once again.

Some clarity came my way one day when Leroy came into the room to tie Jasper's tie. It was the first time I'd ever seen the kid dressed up. Here he was, a little light coming through the window, warming the tone of his skin, making him look tanned and healthy, in a suit, white button-down shirt, and dark tie with little white anchors on it. The suit was a little baggy on him, and since he didn't pull it from *his* closet, I gathered it might have been Leroy's from when he was trimmer. It took Leroy a few tries to get the knot right. "It's hard to do this on someone else's neck," he kept saying. When Leroy finally got it, he brought the knot up into place, adjusted the collar, and dusted off the boy's shoulders. The house was quiet, only a stir of wind outside, and both of them hugged. "I'm just so sorry this happened to you," Leroy said.

Jasper didn't answer, but I could see him crumple into his uncle.

"He was in a lot of pain in prison," Leroy said. "I didn't think it would end up like this for him."

There was a long pause. And neither spoke for a while; some birds cooed and cawed outside. It was as if nature, too, was offering its condolences.

The sun bullied its way through a few clouds and shone hard through the window, lighting the two men in front of me even more than before.

"Your dad was always troubled, J. You know that. But he loved you so much. There's something beautiful about that."

Jasper dug his hands hard into Leroy's dark suit jacket.

I studied them as they left the room. I could still see Jasper's little eyes. His hands were the same as the day I was gifted to him. I mean, sure, they'd grown, but they'd kept their softness and smaller-than-usual nails. His voice had deepened, but it had also kept its sweetness, and his gaze had stayed the same, too—pensive and full of wonder.

The world, however, was making Jasper hard. After a lot of rain, it seemed, he wasn't able to see the sun the same way. He didn't see life as light interspersed with darkness, but rather, I think he saw the default setting of the world as bleak—with just blips of joy to shake things up from time to time.

After the suicide of his father in prison, it was back to the norm for Jasper. He came home from school one day, terribly upset. His face was scarlet, and he sank into the bed. He took a pill from his bag and sat there, atop the comforter, until it took effect.

Then the phone rang and startled him.

Jasper picked it up. "Yes," he said.

"Mr. Wagner," the voice on the other line said.

"Yeah," Jasper said. His voice was groggy and soft from the pill.

"This is Principal Thompson from Lawrence High."

Jasper seemingly understood the importance, and he realized the call was for Leroy, the other Mr. Wagner. "Oh, yes. Hello." He changed the pitch of his voice and pulled the receiver a few inches from his mouth. "Is everything okay?"

246

The principal was fooled and informed Jasper about Jasper, saying that he was often not at school, often showed up late, and wasn't turning in assignments.

"You do know that his father just hung himself in prison, right?" Jasper said.

"We do, yes."

"I mean, Christ."

"True, true," Principal Thompson said.

"I mean, I ain't making excuses for the kid, but seems to me he's trying to survive right now and that reading some books and writing papers ain't exactly the best way to grieve. I'll speak to him, though. Thank you, sir," Jasper said, hanging up the phone.

***

I saw less and less of Jasper in the coming months. He spent a lot of time out of the house, and when he was home, he just came in and passed out on the bed. He no longer prayed or cried. He didn't sleep soundly any longer, either, always tossing and turning, the bed always beaten up in the morning with the comforter crumpled sadly at the base of the bed. No matter how much he slept, he always woke up with pale skin and blueish semicircles under his eyes. His forehead was always greasy, too, and he wore the same coat day after day.

There was a week that he stayed home from school with the flu, and he cried a couple of times, and I rested high above the closet, wishing I could do something. Then, he took a piece of paper from his backpack and scooted to the edge of the bed, where I could see his hand move across the lined paper. I hoped he was going to draw. It had been a while since I'd seen Jasper sketch. The last time I saw him doodle a

247

bunch of flowers without ever picking up the pen, then he got frustrated and ripped it out of his binder and tossed the sheet of paper to the floor, where it fluttered to the carpet in big swoops. The paper stayed there for a few days, and I studied his single line that curved and bent and made this perfect bouquet. I thought it was beautiful.

But no, not this time. He just kept writing, and I glanced at the words when he stood and paced. "I'm sorry," he wrote. "It's been hard. I love you, Mom and Dad. I love you so much, Uncle Leroy."

He then grabbed me. And we headed to the garage where he located the shells near the industrial freezer and loaded me. It wasn't hunting season, though.

And as good as it felt to be held in his hands, I didn't want to leave the home. As much as I complained about not being used, I wanted to go back above the closet.

But we left, and we headed out the back door, down the hill.

There was light snow today, with the weather warm enough to make it melt as it touched the ground, but in the air the white flakes were pretty, sparkling as they fluttered and traced the air, a cold and perfect dust.

We trudged and trudged. And little by little, Jasper began to cry as we made our way over a small creek that curved in a serpentine fashion. We arrived at a tree, one that Jasper used to draw over and over in his room as a boy. He would use pastels for this particular tree. He then stared at the three hills in the distance, each one a little smaller than the other if you looked at them from left to right.

He stopped crying after a couple of minutes and took big breaths like he had learned from Leroy. It

248

reminded me of the breaths he used to take early on when he was learning to shoot, those special Coke-bottle days when we would ride in the pickup.

He then shut his eyes. His fingers convulsed. And all of a sudden, my barrel was pressed against the roof of his mouth. Moisture and heat streamed against my cold steel. And his breath came fast. Inhale, exhale. Inhale, exhale. Leaving almost no time between the two.

He wrapped his finger around my trigger and pressed timidly, with little pressure, then he released me and yanked my barrel from his mouth. His chest heaved, and he began to cough harder and harder before hocking up some phlegm and eventually vomiting.

Thank you, I thought. Please, I thought. Don't do that again, Jasper. I beg you.

But he didn't listen. Before long, I was wedged back into his mouth, and he pressed me hard against the back of his throat, so hard that he gagged, and I was ripped out and back in the open air. Then he cried and took the note out from his coat pocket, balled it up—like he used to do with drawings that displeased him—and tossed it near his boots.

A little gust of wind blew it a few feet from us, and later, another gust pounded and blew it farther and farther, and with each foot the wind put between us and the note, I felt better.

We stayed there under the tree, the wind sighing through the branches. We were both calming down, our nerves steadying with each passing minute. Tears came, and one, actually, fell onto my forestock. The droplet was warmer than I imagined and didn't evaporate in the cold air. Then he tossed me, and I landed a few feet from him.

I was pleased. Yes, I thought. Good. Perfect.

249

It was almost as if I was getting through to him. I thought so hard, concentrated so deeply—and these notions seemingly spurred him. He picked me up, and we began making our way back toward the home.

One, two.

One, two.

His feet plopped on the ground. His tears had dried now, but his eyes were still glassy, almost healthy looking, and his skin, while red just moments ago, had calmed and regained its normal hue.

We were literally headed toward the sun at the moment. And I couldn't believe that such horror and beauty had happened so close together in time. Moments ago, my muzzle had been in his mouth, and now I was being carried safely, diagonally along his chest, toward the warm rays of light.

It would be okay, I thought. He had learned his lesson. He knew, at some point, the world would soften, give once again.

And it was just as I enjoyed this warmness both in thought and sunlight that Jasper slipped.

His right foot struggled to grip some grass, and he fell forward. It happened slowly. We both approached the ground, our 90-degree angle, slowly decreasing. 45. 35. 20.

My barrel came down as we fell, and one of his fingers—in an attempt to break his fall— wrapped around my trigger and fired a round directly into his sternum at point-blank range.

It was a crack that echoed through the valley. A shot that I can still hear, followed by ringing that bounced through and over the terrain for seconds before falling still again. One millisecond that changed both our lives forever.

I lay underneath him, knowing he was dead, feeling his hot blood stream against me. After a long time, the blood stopped coming. Then it turned cold.

It wasn't until hours later that Leroy found us.

He looked dead himself when he finally located Jasper. I heard him calling his name for at least forty minutes before spotting us. "Jasper! Jasper! Jasper. Jasper . . ." His voice seemed to know before he did.

Leroy called the police, and before long, there were many men in dark uniforms blocking off the area and speaking in direct voices.

When they rolled Jasper over, I was taken off the ground and dropped into a plastic bag, obscuring the final image I had of Jasper. I didn't look anywhere from the neck down. I just took in his soft face, closed eyes, and the faintest smile.

It's been three months, and I'm in a warehouse where they keep evidence and guns and drugs and all sorts of documents. It's always dark except for when someone comes in and flips on the lights. They ran all sorts of tests on me and determined, correctly, that Jasper was the victim of an accident.

I guess it's best that way with only me knowing the total truth.

I think a lot these days. That's all there is to do. I imagine the ranch, the sky. I worry about Leroy. And I miss my best friend, Jasper.

ACKNOWLEDGMENTS

To Kyle Newman and Justin Rampy for their love of short fiction and their belief in this collection. I am forever grateful.

To Tim Antonides for being my incredible first reader.

To Maggie Morris for giving this collection shape and clarity.

To Niles Reddick, Chih Wang and Racquel Henry for their steadfast support.

To Sophfronia Scott and T.D. Johnston for their incredible blurbs and love of story.

To the editors and publishers of the following publications where these stories first appeared, some in slightly different form: *New Rivers Press, Hidden Peak Review, The Saturday Evening Post, The Coachella Review, The Blue Mountain Review, ELJ Editions, Short Story America, Marco Polo Magazine, The Hopper, Black Fox Literary Magazine, New World Review, The McNeese Review, Y'all Magazine,* and *Rat World.*

To my incredible friends and family. I wanted to list you all by name, but the fear of leaving someone out—which I did the last time I compiled such a list—breaks my heart too much to bear.

And to you, dear reader. Thank you for the journey and ride we just shared. I hope you will be with me for the next one.

ABOUT THE AUTHOR

MATHIEU CAILLER is the author of seven books: one novel, two short story collections, two volumes of poetry, and two children's titles. His stories, poems, and essays have appeared in over one hundred publications, including the *Saturday Evening Post* and the *Los Angeles Times.* He is the recipient of numerous awards, most notably the Shakespeare Award, the Short Story America Prize, the New England Book Festival Award, the Los Angeles Book Festival Prize, and the Paris Festival Book Prize. Connect with him on social media @writesfromla or at mathieucailler.com.